Alice's unfinished business has caused her and her family a lot of unforeseen aggravation, and Alice seeks to make amends. But it seems life isn't finished with her yet. Just when Alice thinks they're about to be happy again, life throws her one more curve, and this one is a doozy!

A K'Anne Meinel novel

Also by K'Anne Meinel:

Novels in Paperback:

SHIPS *CompanionSHIP, FriendSHIP,*
RelationSHIP
Long Distance Romance
Children of Another Mother
Erotica
The Claim
Bikini's Are Dangerous
The Complete Series
Germanic
Malice Masterpieces 1
The First Five Books
Represented
Timed Romance
Malice Masterpieces 2
Books Six through Ten
The Journey Home
Out at the Inn
Shorts
Anthology Volume 1
Lawyered
Malice Masterpieces 3
Books Eleven through Fifteen
Blown Away
Blown Away
The Alternate Cover

Small Town Angel
Pirated Love
Doctored
Veil of Silence
Malice Masterpieces 4
Books Sixteen through Twenty
The Outsider
Pirated Heart
Recombinant Love
Survivors
Inn the Dog House
Flight
An Island Between Us
Malice Masterpieces 5
Books Twenty-One through Twenty-Five
Malice Masterpieces 6
Books Twenty-Six through Thirty
Beauty and the Beast

Vetted Series:
Vetted
Cavalcade (Prequel)
Pioneering (Prequel)
Vetted Further
Vetted Again

Novellas in Paperback:

Sapphic Surfer
Sapphic Cowgirl
Sapphic Cowboi
Sayyida
The Northwood Lodge

The Malice Series:
Mysterious Malice (Book 1)
Meticulous Malice (Book 2)
Mistaken Malice (Book 3)
Malicious Malice (Book 4)
Masterful Malice (Book 5)
Matrimonial Malice (Book 6)
Mourning Malice (Book 7)
Murderous Malice (Book 8)
Mental Malice (Book 9)
Menacing Malice (Book 10)
Minor Malice (Book 11)
Morally Malice (Book 12)
Morose Malice (Book 13)
Melancholy Malice (Book 14)

Mad Malice (Book 15)
Macabre Malice (Book 16)
Marinating Malice (Book 17)
Macerating Malice (Book 18)
Minacious Malice (Book 19)
Meddlesome Malice (Book 20)
Meandering Malice (Book 21)
Maniacal Malice (Book 22)
Monitoring Malice (Book 23)
Marked Malice (Book 24)
Mandating Malice (Book 25)
Methodical Malice (Book 26)
Malevolent Malice (Book 27)
Militarial Malice (Book 28)
Machiavellian Malice (Book 29)
Malefic Malice (Book 30)

Religious Experience
Lied

All Novels and Novellas in paperback are also available as e-books.

A Woman Down Under Series:

Shanghaied (Prequel)
Outback Born
Outback Bred
Outback Heritage
Outback Native
Outback Splendor
Outback Yearnings (Prequel)
Outback Escape

Pocket Paperbacks:

Mysterious Malice (Book 1)
Sapphic Surfer
Sapphic Cowgirl
Meticulous Malice (Book 2)
Mistaken Malice (Book 3)
Malicious Malice (Book 4)
Masterful Malice (Book 5)
Matrimonial Malice (Book 6)
Mourning Malice (Book 7)
Murderous Malice (Book 8)
Mental Malice (Book 9)
Menacing Malice (Book 10)
Minor Malice (Book 11)
Morally Malice (Book 12)
Morose Malice (Book 13)
Melancholy Malice (Book 14)
Mad Malice (Book 15)
Macabre Malice (Book 16)
Marinating Malice (Book 17)

In E-Book Format:
Short Stories

Fantasy
Wet & Wet Again
Family Night
Quickie ~ Against the Car
Quickie ~ Against the Wall
Quickie ~ Over the Couch
Mile High Club
Quickie ~ Under the Pier
Heel or Heal
Kiss
Family Night 2
Beach Dreams
Internet Dreamers
Snoggered
On the Parkway
Stable Affair
Kept
Stolen
Agitated
Love of my LIFE
Quickie in an Elevator, GOING DOWN?
Into the Garden
The Book Case
The Other Women
Menage a WHAT?

LARGE Print Novels

SHIPS CompanionSHIP, FriendSHIP, RelationSHIP
Erotica Volume 1
Long Distance Romance
Children of Another Mother
Bikini's Are Dangerous
The Complete Series
Malice Masterpieces
The First Five Books
To Love a Shooting Star
The Claim
Represented
Timed Romance

K'ANNE MEINEL

Militarial

Malice

ISBN-13: 978-1959436058

K'Anne Meinel is available for comments at KAnneMeinel@aim.com as well as on Facebook, Google +, or her blog @ http://kannemeinel.wordpress.com/ or on Twitter @ kannemeinelaim.com, or on her website @ www.kannemeinel.com if you would like to follow her to find out about stories and book's releases.

www.shadoepublishing.com

ShadoePublishing@gmail.com

Shadoe Publishing is a United States of America company
Cover by: K'Anne Meinel
Edited by: Deb Amia

Militarial Malice

MILITARIAL MALICE

Book 28

"Madelyn, can you hear me?" Alice called into the phone, only to hear it squawking horribly again. She knew that sound, so she hung up and immediately started typing on her computer. She was quickly firing up another computer to send a cross connection and scramble the signals in the house.

"Alice, what's wrong with my cell phone?" Kathy asked as she brought down a tray with Alice's breakfast. She had the tray in one hand and was holding up her phone with the other, a questioning look on her face.

"Someone is *deliberately* scrambling our signal," she said as she typed rapidly. "Try using it now," she said as Kathy set the tray down on the edge of desk. "Never mind," she said when her own phone started ringing.

"Alice? Did you hang up on me?" Madelyn asked worriedly from across the miles.

"No, someone was listening and scrambled my signal here. I was asking you if it was Senator Ken Edwards' name you found in your information?"

Kathy's head snapped up from where she had been looking at her phone. She knew that name, but she had only heard it in passing, and it had been before she and Alice got together.

"Yes, but how did you–?" Madelyn asked and then stopped herself as she realized who she was talking to.

"Thank you, Madelyn. Your debt is paid." She went to hang up, but the CIA operative stopped her.

"Wait, Alice. I need more…" the woman began, and when Alice heard her, she stopped her finger from disconnecting the call.

"No, Madelyn. We're even. You took too long, and I discovered the information for myself. If anything, I would say you still owe me," Alice pointed out, wanting to bank future points in case she needed a favor. She never knew when that might be necessary.

"I tried–" she began, but Alice interrupted her.

"You failed." They both knew Alice was right.

"Do you want my help with the school–?"

"Already too late on that."

"How about the home invasion?"

Alice knew she was being monitored since the agent had that tidbit of information too. "Again, *too late*."

Madelyn sighed. That tone of voice could mean many things. She knew Alice had more material, and Wolfe was not going to be happy if she didn't get it from her. A lot of Madelyn's job was playing a waiting game,

and all she could do was offer help in exchange for information. "Well, you know I'm here if you need–?"

"Yes, I have *your number*," Alice interjected, smiling at the double entendre and hanging up the call.

"Senator?" Kathy asked as soon as Alice was free.

"Well, senator no more," she pointed out.

"But…?"

"Remember the husband and wife team that were involved with Connie?" Alice asked her wife, watching her reaction to the question.

Connie had been one of the four amigos back in college. There had been Kathy, Portia, Andie, and Connie Weaver, Alice's twin sister. They'd all attended college together at Stanford while Alice went to Harvard back east. The name of Alice's sister invoked a lot of pleasant memories for the now much older woman. Their oldest daughter, Kit, was attending the same college Kathy had attended, and she was having some of the same experiences. "But after all these years?"

"I'm betting that Audi," Alice nodded her head to indicate the car that was parked regularly on the street, "has a triangulation gadget and is scrambling our phones if we mention his name, which just happened. Where's the meter?"

"Will that…?" Kathy started to ask as she went to the bookcase to retrieve the meter.

"No, but I want to sweep the house again. We had a lot of people through here with the home invasion."

Kathy agreed, and with Alice watching, she swept the office. "Wasn't the senator in prison?" she asked as she worked. Alice turned off the router, so it wouldn't send out false signals.

"He might be out," she answered, realizing she hadn't kept up on that situation.

She could see Kathy had finished scanning the TV room and was heading for the exercise room. Alice had spent a lot of time in that room recently, working out and bringing her body back to a level of fitness she had missed. With her weight gain and enforced inactivity, she felt she had been losing muscle mass for a long time. She intended, especially once her leg was healed, to get back into shape and was working daily towards achieving her goal. Her physical therapist had noted the tightening of Alice's muscles all around the leg and worried that she was working the healing limb. Alice assured her she wasn't, and that was the truth. She *had* tried, but it hurt too much.

Kathy returned half an hour later after sweeping the entire house and even taking a walk around the perimeter. The meter hadn't measured any listening devices other than the small night vision cameras they had installed themselves.

"Okay, we can talk," Kathy announced as she placed the device back on its shelf.

Alice looked up from her computer. "Apparently, Ken Edwards got out of jail a few years ago and wants revenge. At least, I think he wants revenge since he seems to be behind the bozos who scrambled our phones when his name was mentioned this morning." She indicated the cell phone and her computers where she had gotten the information that Madelyn just confirmed. "That means they are listening to our phone calls for any sign that we know his name, and *now*, he knows."

"What does that mean?" Kathy asked, but in her heart, which was sinking at the news, she already knew the answer.

"He is going to assume that I am coming for him."

"And are you?"

"I have some research to do first." Alice indicated her computers, then she also pointed at the cast on her leg. It felt like her leg was taking forever to heal, and it was annoying the heck out of her. They hadn't given her a walking cast yet, and she was still forced to hobble around on crutches.

"I wouldn't have thought he'd ever get out of prison," Kathy mused, remembering what little information Alice had mentioned about him over the years. She knew they had all been saddened by the loss of Constance, Connie as she was known to her loved ones. Kathy had often wondered about her friend but never asked Alice about Connie's habit of attracting rich men into her life. Connie's dead body had been dumped in her house, if Kathy recalled correctly. Alice had found her sister, and her subsequent investigation had led to the senator and his wife, also a senator. Apparently, Ken had killed his wife plus Connie and several other women. Kathy wasn't about to bring up that painful memory with Alice, even if she was a bit sketchy on some of the details.

"Well, with *good* behavior, he must have come up for parole," Alice murmured as she thought about the fact that she had missed this detail and allowed the senator live, even if it was in prison. It had been so many years, and she never suspected the man might look her up and cause the disruption in her life she now suspected he was behind. All their problems with the IRS and the police might have been instigated by tips from this man and his friends. She was certain he had influenced all the right people, many who might believe his story that he had been unfairly convicted. Still, he had been a powerful man, and he would have maintained his contacts. Her eyes narrowed as she contemplated what she already knew and what she still had to investigate.

"You think he was involved in the home invasion?"

"No, that wasn't him," Alice said with absolute confidence.

"No? How do you know?"

"Do you *really* want to know?" Alice asked, raising a brow and wondering if this was going to be the straw that broke the camel's back for her wife. They had been working on repairing their marriage, and they had to do something about the divorce, or the courts would dissolve the paperwork, and they'd be back at square one if they wanted to proceed after all.

Kathy thought about the question and nodded. It was important that she know what was coming that might affect their family. She should prepare herself for it, so she could do what she needed to protect them. Alice was good at solving this sort of thing. She'd take the battle to them and their enemies.

"Remember Sebastian?" Alice asked conversationally, leaning back in her chair with her leg propped on a footstool. Her leg was itching again, which supposedly meant it was healing. She was certain the itching was caused by the dark hairs she could see growing in the cast as well as all the castoff skin that was building up from the daily shedding her leg was doing as it healed. She'd seen what her foot looked like the last few times they'd changed the cast; it was gross with the buildup of dead skin at the bottom.

"Isn't he dead?" Kathy asked, thinking she'd heard Alice mention that.

Alice nodded as she remembered the funeral she had attended before her accident. "He left an heir, and I believe his heir may have had his people pay us a visit. I'll be looking into that when this is better," her hand swept across her leg indicating the cast and the underlying break.

Kathy nodded. That home invasion had been terrifying, not knowing if the men were going to physically hurt them or the children. Fortunately, the ten thousand dollars in their safe had seemed to satisfy the men. What she really hated was how their assault had affected Emily, who was now obsessed with defending herself and never allowing herself to become a victim again. Kathy knew Emily was reacting more to the betrayal of Carmen and her other friends than the home invasion, but having that man touch her had really frightened the young teen.

Had Kathy known what the men were saying about their daughter, she'd have been even more furious. Alice had understood their Russian comments and knew Kathy would have been just as murderous in her thoughts as Alice was when she heard them.

Alice had a lot of planning to do, and her leg was hampering her physically and mentally. In her mind, these people were already dead. It was just a matter of how and when Alice would bring about their deaths. She turned back to her 'research' on the computers.

* * * * *

It had been months since Alice broke her leg in the landslide on Malibu's Pacific Coast Highway. As Kathy drove her to check on her house, Alice looked over where the hillside had come down. She saw very few signs of the mud and rocks that had rained down and enveloped her Ferrari that night. The insurance had paid for the expensive sports car but only time would heal the injuries. There were no signs left on her skin of the bruising the rocks had caused, and the abrasions had long ago healed, so the cast on her leg was the only remaining evidence of the long-ago near tragedy.

"Penny for your thoughts?" Kathy asked, seeing Alice so still. She wasn't agitated, which would have been a better sign.

"I'm thinking that California does a good job of erasing things," she admitted cryptically.

Kathy gulped. Although she knew Alice had justified the many killings she had committed over the years—hell, Kathy had participated in several of them—she still couldn't get past the fact that her wife was a serial killer. She wasn't your *average* serial killer with a pattern or a compulsion to kill. It was more like her justification to right the wrongs of her world. Now, according to what Kathy knew, there were a couple more people in Alice's crosshairs, and it was only her broken leg that was preventing her from carrying out even more killings. Kathy always worried that Alice would screw up and get caught, and then, she would have to watch as her wife was given the electric chair or a lethal injection for her crimes. Alice wasn't perfect. She had complained about getting older, but so far, they had been very, *very* lucky that she hadn't been caught.

The house in Malibu was in order. It was a bit musty from the windows being closed and locked, but nothing seemed out of the ordinary. They opened the windows while they were there to catch a cross breeze. They'd brought the meter to test the house for bugs and found nothing. Apparently, since Alice's main residence had moved back to Palos Verdes, so had her followers. Madelyn had gotten the FBI to stop tailing her, but she could do nothing about Ken Edwards' flunkies. If Alice had asked her for that favor, she would have used her position in the CIA to make it stop, but Alice wouldn't ask. They both knew Alice would handle it herself in her own unique way. Already, Madelyn had people watching the ex-senator, who was now some sort of motivational speaker earning a pittance compared to the hundreds of thousands, maybe even millions, he had

earned back in his days as a senator alongside his wife. They had been the golden couple and were compared to the likes of the Kennedys. Their deviant lifestyle had been the death of them after they killed Alice Weaver's sister, Constance.

"Why don't you put this place on the market?" Kathy asked as Alice clumped around checking the less obvious locks she had installed versus the locks that were blatantly obvious to the casual observer. She shut the windows again and made sure their locks were in good shape.

Alice stood up, balancing on her crutches as she looked at her wife "in name only." They had yet to become physically intimate again since Kathy had asked her for a divorce so many months ago. "I don't think we're there yet, are we?"

Kathy flushed. So much had gone on in their lives since Alice's accident, and they hadn't yet moved beyond the point of being anything other than housemates, although the children were happier they were all under the same roof. Even Kit had commented on it when she came home for visits, but they weren't yet wives in every sense of the word. "No, not yet. I guess not," she admitted ruefully and let the subject drop.

Alice climbed the much steeper stairs of her house, one awkward step at a time, and she checked all the rooms on the second floor. Glancing at the unused gaming set-up gave her an idea, and she fired it up as she continued looking around the other rooms. She was checking for something…anything out of place. When she returned to the gaming room, she also started up a game she had enjoyed with her son, one that allowed instant messaging between the players. She left a cryptic message for someone on the game, which would set something in motion and would be waiting for her when she chose to return and receive her own messages. It was something she had set up previously as a safeguard to

avoid being watched. Many people were watching her, but they were looking at the more obvious computers, which Alice Weaver and her investments were known for. After shutting down the game and the gaming computers, she made sure everything else was off in her son's room before she carefully descended the stairs and found her wife looking out at the gorgeous Malibu beach. It was a cold, brisk spring day, but the sky was clear and sunny with no signs of rain. The wind had blown away the storm clouds and people were taking advantage of this break in the weather to walk the beach.

"This is such a pretty view," Kathy commented as she heard Alice and her crutches clumping up behind her.

"Yes, it is," Alice admitted, looking out.

They didn't need to say more. They'd been married a long time and understood what the other was thinking without spoken words. It was a comfortable silence each had missed in her own way, not realizing until that moment they hadn't had it for a while. Being together like this and enjoying the beauty together was enough…for now.

As they drove home with the ever-present Audi behind them, Kathy got mad and sped up.

"Careful there, Mario," Alice teased, wishing she was behind the wheel.

"Why can't they just leave us alone?" Kathy lamented angrily. She passed several people only to find herself stuck at the back of a long line of cars. The Audi effortlessly kept up with them, allowing just enough distance between the cars that it would not be obvious to the casual observer. Alice was not a casual observer and Kathy was aware of them now too.

Alice waited to confirm that the Audi was passing some of the same cars Kathy had passed. "Pull onto this road *NOW!*" she told Kathy suddenly.

Surprised, Kathy instinctively listened to her wife and spun the wheel, nearly cutting someone off and causing a pedestrian that had been about to cross the street that intersected with PCH to pull back in alarm.

"Go down there and quickly back into the first driveway," Alice pointed. She looked back to see if the Audi had seen where they turned.

Kathy was busy doing what Alice had commanded. She was amused at this game of cat and mouse. She too wished Alice was driving, but she had really enjoyed that Alice relied on her to cart her around to appointments and such. She only regretted that Alice wasn't yet in good enough shape to stop the people who had been following her for so long. She remembered how impressed she was when Alice broke the undercover officers' window with a rock when they were watching the women's house.

They both sat in the car and listened to the engine humming quietly as they waited…and waited. Eventually, the Audi sped past them on its way down the road. "Wait…" Alice cautioned, putting her hand on Kathy's arm when she seemed about to put the car in gear. She waited two minutes before she let go of Kathy's arm and nodded. Kathy inched out of the drive she had backed into and looked both ways, but she saw no sign of the Audi.

"You know, they'll just go to the house in Palos Verdes and wait for us?" she asked dryly.

"Yeah, but it will unnerve them that we got away so easily," Alice pointed out with a laugh. "It's a head game, which I think is overdue. Why don't we stay away for a while? Is Mrs. Fernandez at the house

today?" At Kathy's nod, Alice asked, "Why don't we go out for dinner? I'm sure the kids will be okay if they come home and we're not there."

Kathy was thrilled with the idea. It had been a very long time since she had been on a date with Alice. They were both dressed casually. Alice wore her ripped pants that fit over her cast and a jean-jacket with a t-shirt underneath, and Kathy had on casual jeans and a quilted jacket over a button-down shirt. "Where should we go?"

"How about a drive-in?"

"Theater?" Kathy asked, confused.

"No, something like Sonic or another fast-food place, if you prefer. Surely, Los Angeles has plenty of drive-ins like that around."

They ended up going to the drive-in chain, Sonic, where they both had bright, colorful drinks, hamburgers, and fries. They talked like they had in the olden days. It had been a long time since they treated themselves to a date, and they both thoroughly enjoyed it. It was quite late when they arrived home, and the familiar Mercedes was waiting at the side of the road in place of the Audi. The two occupants tried to duck and avoid the headlights of the Lexus and failed. Alice laughed at her watchers as she and Kathy drove by, the gates of the Palos Verdes estate closing firmly behind the sporty Lexus.

* * * * *

Director Wolf was not a happy man. They had invested months of investigation using teams of people in cooperation with the FBI, and they hadn't gotten much on the people that Alice Weaver had brought them. Yes, they had reams of paperwork on these families and extensive biographies, but the only thing these people had in common was they were

all wealthy, linked to the mob, and dead. Try as they might, they had found no proof that Alice Weaver or Sasha Brenhov were connected to those deaths. Some of the properties these people had previously owned were now owned by the Brenhov holdings, but that was inconclusive. Some of the properties had been owned before, so there could have been a sale and a resale. The agency simply didn't know. None of the evidence they had tied any of it to Alice Weaver except superficially. She was thought to have been in the company of the Russian woman, but that didn't prove anything. There were no signs of the enormous wealth that Brenhov had. Alice Weaver was back with her wife, so their combined wealth was reasonable and now in line with the IRS after the deal they had cut. It was all provable wealth. He hated that! He was certain she was dirty! Madelyn Korbel was no help either. He suspected she somewhat admired the woman who had blackmailed the CIA and by association, the United States government.

"Did you give this information to Alice Weaver?" he indicated the file containing the name of a former senator. Ken Edwards was a widower, who supported himself with speaking engagements these days. He had gone to prison for the death of his wife and Constance Weaver, the sister of Alice Weaver. That fact alone raised eyebrows in their investigation. It was too much of a coincidence to believe there wasn't tit for tat going on here. Someone wanted revenge.

"No, sir," she admitted to him.

"You didn't? Didn't you promise her—?" he asked, pleased that maybe she was finally on board and ready to help thwart this mysterious woman.

"No, sir. Alice *gave me* the senator's name, and I confirmed it," she clarified.

"What do you mean she gave it to you?!"

"Somehow, she had already uncovered that information, and she wasn't going to wait for us to give her the name of who had had her investigated." Madelyn waited for him to blow his top. If he really thought about it, this meant they still owed Alice. It had taken them months to ferret out information that Alice had probably gotten in weeks. Whatever her sources of information were, they shouldn't be superior to that of the Central Intelligence Agency or the Federal Bureau of Investigation.

"What's this I hear about her kid being involved in child pornography?" Wolf asked, changing the subject and dismissing some key evidence he had overlooked.

"Emily was the victim, not the perpetrator," she told him. "It's in this report here that Givens had sorted. The feds are looking into the situation because it crossed state lines."

He sighed. This was just one more thing about this Weaver woman that was hinky. "She didn't divorce her wife?"

Madelyn shook her head. "Apparently not, sir. Since the accident where she broke her leg, she's been living back in the Palos Verdes home." This information proved they were still keeping tabs on Alice, but then, he had ordered it. While the FBI had been pulled off the surveillance, there were other means for watching a subject.

"What about the Malibu house?"

"Empty, sir."

"Must be nice to be able to afford that kind of waste," he mumbled, pretending to look at one of his reports. Madelyn knew he was faking it because the report was upside down.

"Was there anything else?" she asked, wanting to get back to work. She had dozens of cases besides Alice Weaver's on her desk.

"Yeah, sure. Dismissed," he waved her off and sat down, thinking about these developments and wondering what Alice Weaver would do with the information. Trying to bypass Madelyn, he discovered she was already ahead of him and had the former senator under surveillance. He smiled. She was good…she was *very* good.

* * * * *

"Okay, Alice. This is the day you've been waiting for. Now, this walking cast is just for *walking*. You are not to be run in it, which would crush it. Walk only! And you still can't get it wet. I know you've been walking on this," she indicated the cast they had just sawed off, "because the bottom is filthy." It was obvious Alice had turned it into a walking cast. "Please try to be careful and restrain yourself in this new cast. Also, no lifting weights with this leg *yet*," Doctor Bryant warned her. The doctor knew that Alice had tried to be patient about the delays, but there had been so many complications. The pins and the breaks had been complex, and it had taken an extraordinary amount of time for them to heal.

Alice tried out the walking cast, using the wall, the counter, and her wife to maintain her balance. "Should I keep the crutches?" Alice asked the doctor, feeling not too thrilled at how unsteady she was; she had thought the new cast would act like a brace.

"No, let's try this cane," the doctor offered one to her. "This should help with your balance."

Alice liked how the cane looked, and it did help her keep her balance and avoid falling flat on her face. She had to go slow, but she could keep

going. She nodded. "How long will I have to wear this?" she asked, indicating the new cast.

"As long as it takes," Doctor Bryant answered cryptically with a smile. She knew how impatient Alice was. She wanted to be running, but her leg simply wasn't up to it yet. Alice had asked the physical therapist about getting her leg back in shape and eventually jogging or running, and the therapist has reported that conversation to the doctor. They had all noticed the increased muscle tone throughout the rest of her body.

Alice had even gone so far as submerging her last cast in the bathtub deliberately, so they were forced to put on a new one. The wetness had soaked into the cotton and remained against her leg and foot until they could fit her in for a last-minute appointment. They'd had to peel off all the dead skin, leaving the foot cold, vulnerable, and itchy as it dried out in the exposed air. Fortunately, the leg was healing well, if a bit slow. "Look at that!" Alice exclaimed, pointing to the long, dark hairs. "I'm blonde, and my hairs shouldn't look like that!"

"Well, as you get older–" the doctor tried to tell her, but Alice wasn't having any of that.

"I had all that hair removed with a laser years ago. Why is it reappearing now?"

"It's not as thick as you think it is. It's just noticeable because you aren't used to seeing it, and your skin is white without your summer tan."

Alice was annoyed. She couldn't shave it, and she certainly couldn't pluck that many hairs. "I tell you, when this cast comes off, I'm making an appointment with the laser hair removal people. They better remove this hair once and for all, or they're going to refund me for the expensive treatments I paid for all those years ago!"

"Your body has changed as you have aged," Doctor Bryant told her. "You must have noticed some changes?"

Alice had to admit the doctor was right but excess body hair was not something she wanted to deal with. She'd have it zapped at the first opportunity.

Kathy thought it was hilarious. Alice was always so fastidious, and she had carefully groomed her body over the years. In fact, when they met, Alice had helped Kathy change her style of clothing, get rid of unattractive outfits, and learn how to keep herself impeccably. As a result of Alice's teachings, she felt better and was more confident.

* * * * *

Using her new cane, Alice and Kathy, accompanied by Nia Toyomota and Portia, entered an office in downtown Los Angeles for a meeting with the Pasternacks and their lawyer. They had come to sign a settlement and avoid dragging their case through the courts. The Pasternacks' homeowner insurance was paying most of the settlement amount, and Alice had to wonder how much was actually coming out of these people's pockets. Emily had let slip that Carmen was using her mother's being cut of work as an excuse for why she had been acting up, but they weren't buying it.

"Well, if you'll sign here and here and here," the Pasternacks' attorney stated, but Nia held up her hand and quickly reviewed the paperwork. When she was done, she showed the paperwork to Portia, who also quickly glanced over the papers they had prepared before nodding and allowing Alice and Kathy to sign. A cashier's check was then passed across the wide table and everyone rose.

"I am sorry for everything that happened," Sandi stated, holding out her hand to Kathy. Richard held out his hand to Alice, who took it begrudgingly.

"Ouch!" Kathy exclaimed, pulling her hand back quickly.

"Oh, I'm sorry. It's this old ring of mine. It catches on things sometimes," Sandi said, but her apology sounded insincere to Alice's ears. When Sandi held her hand out to Alice, she refused. Alice held her hands up high and gave a slight laugh, and Sandi realized Alice wasn't going to shake her hand. Her eyes narrowed fractionally, but she laughed it off with good grace while exchanging a look with her husband.

They all left the building, Nia and Portia with their clients in one elevator, and the others using a second elevator in the highrise. "Well, that's that, and I'll head over to our offices to file these," Nia stated, patting her briefcase where she had placed the signed documents. The Pasternacks' attorney also had duplicate copies for their records. "Hopefully, I won't hear from *them* again," she indicated the defendants, who had arrived in the lobby more quickly than they had.

"And the other lawsuits?" Alice joked. They all knew those other suits might take years since not everyone was willing to settle. Still, it kept the lawyers busy, and Alice didn't mind. Nia had enjoyed the trip out to California, and she was considering an offer to run the office out here but before she made a decision, she had to discuss it with her wife.

* * * * *

"Mom, you're walking!" Emily greeted them when they arrived at the house. She was coming up from downstairs, where it looked like she had

been working out. She was wearing sweats, a tank top, a sports bra, and looked a little sweaty.

"Yep, I'm crutch-free, for now," she answered with a smile although Kathy was carrying the crutches just in case. They'd paid for them in full, so they might as well keep them.

"I'm putting these in here," Kathy indicated the hall closet.

"Hopefully, I will never need them again," Alice put in as she slowly headed for the kitchen, where she found Sean and one of his friends wolfing down a tremendous amount of food. "Hi, there," she said by way of greeting.

"Oh, hi, Mom. This is Greg, and we're just catching a snack," Sean told her.

"A snack?" she laughed as Kathy came up behind her. Their snack looked like it was enough to feed a small nation.

"Yeah, we needed sustenance while we studied. You know, finals," he told her as he shoved half a Twinkie in his mouth and washed it down with half a glass of milk.

"Manners," Kathy cautioned him, not liking how he was shoving the food into his mouth. That would have given her heartburn or choked her

"Which test are you studying for?" Alice asked, amused by her son. He was growing so big and strong, and it amazed her that he had her genes and had come out of Kathy.

"Calculus," both boys mumbled, their mouths filled with food.

"Oooh, gross," Emily said as she came into the kitchen. No one was sure if she was grossed out by the food they had in their mouths or the subject matter.

"C'mon, guys. Manners?" Alice put in, seeing them through the eyes of a parent.

Both boys grabbed napkins and hid behind them as they chewed with their mouths open until they could finally close them and finish chewing. Alice rolled her eyes and turned away, trying to hide a smile from Kathy.

* * * * *

"Alice, I think you should come upstairs," Kathy began hesitantly.

"Did I forget something?" she asked, looking up from the computer information she was examining, trying to gather as much material as she could. There were some things that weren't going to be public knowledge, such as motives and manipulations, but there were other ways she could get the data she needed. She wanted a complete dossier on all the people she was investigating.

Kathy nearly laughed. With a twinkle in her eye, she said, "If we are ever going to make this a proper marriage again," she started, referring to their interrupted conversation earlier that week, "I think we should start sleeping together. Don't you agree?"

Alice tilted her head. "Are you ready for everything that entails? Do you understand what that means? I haven't changed. Circumstances may have changed," her hands encompassed her casted leg, the new computers, and the problems she was working on, "but it's the same shit with different players."

Kathy sighed. She hated being reminded that their life was in a constant state of drama. "I know, but I want to somehow move past all this shit," she spread her hands this time to gesture towards the computers Alice was so diligently working at, "and have a life of our own."

"Do you realize what I'm going to do to these people?" Alice asked, pointing out the obvious.

"I thought you were going to wait until–" she started to say and stopped herself abruptly when Emily walked out of the exercise room.

"What are you two talking about?" she asked, her chest heaving.

Alice was used to hearing her daughter working out in there, using the machines and watching YouTube videos to learn karate. Alice had seen on the video feed from the house that Emily was getting the basic moves, but there were little nuances that were missing, and only a good teacher could impart those things to her. Remembering her own teachers, Alice inwardly shuddered. "Were you eavesdropping?" she asked, sounding amused.

"Not deliberately," she responded, suddenly worried. She knew a few things she shouldn't, and she would have liked to talk to her moms about it, but Kathy always stopped her. And when she approached her, Alice just referred her back to Kathy.

The moms exchanged a look; Kathy looked worried.

"I'm just doing research," Alice told her daughter. She wasn't lying. She stared her down, waiting to see if she would challenge her.

"Mom, I think we both know that's beyond mere research," she said exasperatedly.

Alice didn't answer. She merely stared at her daughter and waited.

"Have you been working out, honey?" Kathy asked into the silence, trying to distract the teen.

"Mom, don't do that. I know you don't think I'm an adult yet, but I'm not stupid," she added. "I know you're planning something," she gestured towards Alice and her computers. "I wish you'd train me to defend myself, so I could help."

"Absolutely not!" both women said at the same time, then looked at each other and laughed.

Em rolled her eyes and shook her head. She couldn't fight both her mothers. She knew it was Kathy's decision and Alice would follow her lead. She also suspected Alice might teach her to defend herself, if the decision was left up to her. Then again, seeing Alice's laser-focused eyes watching her, maybe not, despite the laughter. "C'mon, Mom. Can't I at least take lessons at a dojo?"

Alice looked at Kathy, waiting for her to make the decision. She wouldn't interfere on this one. She knew the kid was desperate for direction because she had heard her crying a couple times when she didn't think anyone could hear her. If she could have, Alice would have gone to the girl and comforted her. Listening to her daughter cry only made her more determined to even the score with the people who caused her pain. Since Alice wasn't yet physically ready to exact revenge, she was taking the time to plan her future moves with military precision. She had maps of Sebastian's properties, those now controlled by others and those owned by Artum and his associates. From what she could glean, Artum was acquiring more properties, not very discreetly either. His holding company was almost too obvious, even though he had layered it in several trusts and other poorly named companies.

"Honey, you're doing fine on your own," Kathy answered, moving over to put her arm around her daughter and ruffle her hair.

"Mom!" Em said, twisting out of her mother's grasp and standing at arm's length. "That's just it. I don't know what I'm doing! YouTube isn't enough." She turned back to Alice. She had seen her stretch and work out, maybe not to the full extent of her abilities, but the little she had seen over the years told her Alice knew what she was doing. Em reached out to her. "You know stuff. Why can't you teach me?"

Alice glanced at Kathy, who looked hurt by the question and by the fact that her little girl didn't want to be held by her. "I don't know if this is the right time," Alice began, earning a glare from Kathy. "I'm laid up, and you're–"

"Too young?! Is that what you were going to say? What if those men come back? I heard that sometimes they wait until the insurance company pays for the damages and replaces the things they stole, and then they come back to steal from you again."

"Who told you that?" Kathy asked, shocked.

Alice watched the exchange between her wife and youngest daughter. She was worried about that too, and the fact that her leg had taken so long to heal hadn't helped her impatience.

"My friends?" she began, but there was a hint of doubt in her voice, and Alice zeroed in on that.

"Which friends?" Alice asked. "You haven't mentioned making any new friends at your new school," she offered, giving the teen an out. She could tell the question had unnerved the teen.

Em started to squirm, wishing she hadn't pushed things. Now, they would know.

"Which friends?" Kathy asked in a kinder tone, watching her switch from leg to leg in her desire to get away. It was obvious the teen was uncomfortable.

Em looked away from her moms, looking everywhere in the room but towards them. Finally, her eyes settled on the floor, and she mumbled something.

"What was that?" Alice asked, waiting for the answer she already knew was coming. She'd begun watching the kid's activities again and had been waiting for something like this. Em had complained about lagging

computer speed a few times, but in fact, it was Alice deleting some things she shouldn't be saying to her friends, especially on the internet. Alice was fast, but she wasn't that fast. She also wasn't always on her computer, and the logs she saw annoyed her when she realized that her daughter was still friends with undesirable people.

"Carmen," she said in a soft voice.

"You're still in contact with her?" Kathy asked, alarmed. She glanced up at Alice.

"She said she was sorry," Em answered defensively.

"Are you aware that those pictures of you are out there forever? No matter if the feds investigate the people that download those pictures of you, they will have pictures of your body and your face forever." Alice pointed out, watching as her wife flinched, and the girl cringed. "That is the friend who heedlessly shared your pictures around school…the school you can no longer attend because of your humiliation."

"She didn't think, and her mom was stressed, and she was upset–"

"That doesn't matter! She did that to her *best* friend," Kathy pointed out, angry at the teen for being so foolish.

"Are you aware that your so-called friend has been encouraging others to share the pictures?" Alice asked. She would have stood up, but her leg was pulsing as her anger with the teen caused her blood to boil. She was holding herself steady, showing no sign of her agitation as she sat behind the desk.

"How do you know that?" Em asked, aghast and willing to defend her friend to her parents.

"Because the twit puts things up in a public forum where anyone can see it," Alice lied cheerfully. She didn't tell her daughter that she'd sent the little bitch a song purportedly from Emily, which contained a backdoor

virus. Now, she had a keylogger as well other software she could use to spy on Carmen, and she had seen what the girl was up to. It had taken a lot of hours to find out what the foolish girl was up to because she was a social butterfly, but Alice felt it was worth every minute. She reached into a drawer and pulled out a disk, flinging it across the room at her daughter like a Frisbee. "Here, look at what your *friend* has been posting about you. She's using you in order to get more information, so she can laugh at you and disparage you further."

"Alice," Kathy said warningly, but neither of them heard her. Similar eyes were staring at each other: one giving off hurt, the other, lightening sharp anger.

"She wouldn't..." Emily began, but her words lacked conviction. Yes, Carmen had been nasty to others, even occasionally, to her friends. Now, Em fingered the crystal disk case thoughtfully. "Where'd you get this?"

"I told you, she's a twit and posts things publicly. You are being duped, and I know you are smarter than that. Wake up, Emily! That girl hurt you." Her hands spread in a gesture encompassing their house. "She hurt your whole family, and she isn't stopping. Some people just can't resist hurting others. They are so self-absorbed they think they must strike first before someone, anyone, does it to them."

"I wouldn't–" she began, aghast at what Alice was telling her.

"Look at that," Alice gestured to the disk her daughter was holding. "*She* would. No, you wouldn't do that because your mother and I brought you up with values and ideals, but there are people out there that don't have any, at least, not the same values and ideals you were taught." She didn't tell the teen that she'd been investigating the Pasternacks and learned Richard was involved with dirty money, but she'd suspected that would be the case since he was involved with Sebastian and Artum. Sardi

wasn't much better. Twelve of her last fifteen patients had died sooner rather than later, and the other three…well, those cases had ended up in the hospital, and they had also eventually died. Being involved in end-of-life care and hospice meant that someone like Sandi could operate with impunity, if she was careful. Remembering how Sebastian had looked and what he had told her, as well as her own observations from meeting the woman, Alice was convinced that Sandi was a killer.

Emily didn't want to believe her mother, but she knew Alice wouldn't lie to her, although she suspected she often bent the truth. Now, she just wanted to escape their scrutiny, so with a huff, she took the disk and headed for the steps.

Kathy waited until she heard the teen slam her door upstairs before asking, "Did you have to tell her that way?"

"Yes, I did. We must stop molly-coddling her. She deserves the truth. She's already hurt and angry. If I could, I would teach her the basics of karate. That twit went so far as suggesting that someone should *do something* about Emily Weaver, implying they should attack her physically. Why? All because Emily didn't like her naked body being plastered all over the internet and all over her high school. Did Emily deserve that?" She waited for Kathy to answer, and when she didn't, she went on. "Our daughter has been irreparably hurt. All we can do is try to make it slightly better. We sent her to another high school because she didn't want to face those people, but she has seen them. She's reached out to them," she gestured to her computers. "They aren't going to leave her alone either."

"So, what do you suggest? We turn her into…you?" Kathy asked angrily.

"No, I don't want that. I just want her to be able to defend herself, only if it becomes physical, of course. She's doing okay, but she lacks finesse and certain techniques…."

"You've been watching her?"

"Of course, I've been watching her. I have nothing else to occupy my time," her hands gestured to the computers again as she answered the last question sarcastically. "I love our children as much as you do, and I'm trying to protect them. That's what I do best."

"Are you saying I don't or wouldn't protect our children?" Kathy asked angrily. So much for inviting Alice back to her bed. This had gone from bad to worse quickly.

"You absolutely would," Alice assured her angry, prickly wife. "You are also the one that nurtured them and taught me how to do that too."

Surprised, Kathy blinked at the back-handed compliment. She calmed a little. "What are we to do?"

"You know what we are going to have to do…eventually."

Kathy turned white. She whispered furiously, "You aren't talking about killing a teenage girl, are you?"

Alice was surprised, and her eyes flared as she pulled back slightly, almost as though she had been hit. "No! Not at all!" she assured her wife. "I'm saying we teach Em to defend herself both physically and mentally. She needs some toughening up, and that's why I gave her the disk. It contains carefully selected items to prove that her *friend* is setting her up yet again and will continue to do so, if she continues that unfortunate friendship. I wish to God she had never become Carmen's friend."

Kathy was relieved. "I'm not ready for you to teach her. The little you told me of your teachers…."

"I would never use those techniques on *our* daughter," Alice assured her, not wishing to discuss her own instructors or the fear she had lived in for a long time until she became good enough to fight back. She wouldn't do that to Emily...ever.

Kathy was further relieved and relaxed a little. "How bad–?" she began to ask, wondering about the disk, when she heard Emily's bedroom door open. She must have flung it open. The sound of the door hitting the wall was loud, and the teen came running down two sets of stairs into the office.

"Is that all really true?" the anguished teen asked, pointing towards her bedroom where her computer contained the files Alice had put on the disk.

"You couldn't possibly have read all that," Alice commented dryly, knowing exactly what was on it.

"No, but the little I did read was horrible!" She started to cry. "She's awful!"

Alice nodded, wishing she could get up quickly to comfort her daughter, but Kathy was there and pulled the unresisting teen into her arms. Alice rose and grabbed her cane to hobble over. Emily was surprised and pleased to feel both her mothers embracing her as she sobbed out her hurt.

"I want to die," she said through her tears, her body shaking as she experienced another shock.

Kathy exchanged a look with Alice, wishing she could take away the hurt.

"I want *her* to die," she said, and Alice looked meaningfully at Kathy, shaking her head. She would never kill a child, no matter how evil she was.

Kathy wished she could wake up. Getting the kids off to school was exhausting her. She was glad it was nearly the end of the school year. Taking Emily to her school and then doubling back to drop Sean at his school when he couldn't catch a ride with a friend, was becoming too much. They had a lot of activities planned for summer, one of which was a surprise trip Alice had planned for the family that included Kit. The trip encompassed two weeks of camping in Sequoia National Park and then on to Yosemite, necessitating the rental of an RV and lots of secret plans. Kit had loved every moment of the planning. Sean would graduate next year and go on to college. He was already being scouted and might get a scholarship for football or basketball. They were all justifiably proud.

"Finally, this damn thing is off!" Alice said as she put on the boot the doctor had given her. It was her first time not wearing a cast in months. What had begun as a need for eight weeks of wearing the infernal walking cast had turned into eighteen weeks. She was finally done with the cast but had to continue physical therapy to regain the strength in her leg. She also had an appointment with the laser surgery place she had used long ago to remove her regrowth of leg hair. Apparently, as she became perimenopausal, the hairs were growing back, nowhere else so splendidly as on her leg where the break had occurred.

"I thought laser surgery killed the follicles and the roots, so I wouldn't ever have hair growing here again?" she had asked when she called for the appointment.

"The human body is a wonderous thing and heals itself marvelously. It's been more than seven years and your body does regenerate itself," the staff member pointed out. Alice had been annoyed but made the

appointment to have the hair removed once again. She knew it might take several sessions, and they would charge her accordingly.

* * * * *

"Are you going to buy a car?" Kathy asked, still loving the fact that Alice was depending on her to be driven everywhere. It gave them an opportunity to talk privately without the children. They had started sleeping together again, but it wasn't very good sex. It was almost like Alice wasn't trying. The passion they had both enjoyed in the past wasn't as intense. The doctor said the things Alice's body had been through—the starvation and other extremes she wouldn't elaborate on—were causing her to go through early menopause, and that was causing all sorts of changes to her body. Kathy wasn't surprised to learn that reduced sex drive was just one of many symptoms of perimenopause.

"You don't want to drive me around in this?" Alice asked, caressing the dash of the lovely Lexus. It really was an attractive car, and now that summer was approaching, they could ride with the top down. Alice liked the car, but she realized she really did need one of her own.

Kathy preened, knowing she had bought a nice, luxurious car they both enjoyed. It wasn't as fancy or expensive as the Porsches that Alice had owned in the past, and it certainly wasn't in the same class as the Ferrari Alice had owned for a short a time, but it was a beautiful car. "C'mon, there are things you are gonna want to do with your own car," Kathy pointed out in a laugh.

Alice agreed. "What kind of car do you think I should get?" she asked, pleased that Kathy wasn't offended.

They discussed various cars they had owned over the years and then, Kathy blurted out, "Not another Ferrari!"

Alice laughed. No, that car had been totally impractical for her.

"What about an SUV?" Kathy asked, remembering the Nissan and the Jeeps Alice had previously owned and wondering about the storage units. She speculated that Alice had begun hiding those sorts of things from her again since she had taken over the finances. Kathy was pretty sure though, that Alice hadn't returned to the house in the valley for a long time.

"Well, it would certainly be more practical than a sports car," Alice mused, thinking about the sports cars she had owned and what she would need now. She'd loved the feel of her Porsche over the years, especially their power, but they were too distinctive. She really could have both a Porsche and SUV, if she was so inclined. She wasn't.

Alice ended up buying a Land Rover Sport based on her son's research. It was almost as though he was trying to make up for past behaviors. He'd surprised her when she'd indicated she was in the market for an SUV. He'd suggested Porsche, Maserati, and a few other vehicle manufacturers. She hadn't even known they made SUVs. She test-drove the different Land Rovers, but she hadn't liked the older, boxy-looking ones. When Sean brought her the specs on the Sport, he had apologized for its $68,000 price tag. But by the time Alice had added several upgrades, it was even more expensive. She'd refused the red color that looked sexy hot, wanting a more nondescript vehicle for what she knew she would be doing in the coming months.

"I like this," Kathy said, settling back into the new SUV's upholstery and looking over all the gadgets on the dash.

"It's nice, isn't it?" Alice agreed.

"Can I drive it?" Emily asked from the back seat as they headed out on a pleasure drive.

"Not for another year," Alice warned her, laughing at her daughter, her eyes twinkling in the rear-view mirror.

"Half a year," her daughter corrected her, feeling pouty at the reference to her age. She had, after all, driven the RAV for her mother once.

"What about me?" Sean asked, sounding a little defensive. After all, he had gotten his driver's permit.

"I think you can use the RAV, now and again," Kathy put in before an argument started. "Let your mom enjoy her new car. She still has to get used to its power," Kathy teased. The new vehicle had power, but it was nothing like the over-priced sports cars she had previously owned.

"I think this will suit me fine," Alice stated, glancing in the rear-view mirror at the car following them and sighing.

The family went out for dinner, the four of them pretending it was like old times and succeeding at the farse. Both moms knew it wasn't as good as the old times. They were aware they were being observed, but for the kid's sakes, they weren't about to spoil their time together.

* * * * *

"What are you doing?" Emily asked as she came up behind Alice quietly. She'd been practicing in the exercise room and was pleased when Alice flinched in surprise.

"Snuck up on me, didn't you?" Alice asked, unable to hide the weapons she was working with. She froze instead, wishing her daughter would just turn and walk away.

"Is that a bow and arrow?" Em asked, surprised when she realized she wasn't quite right. "That's a crossbow," she corrected herself as she walked farther into the office where Alice was working. "Can I try it?" she asked as she reached for one of the shortened arrows, and Alice pulled them out of her reach.

"No, I don't think your mc–" she began just as Kathy entered the office. She sighed. She was so busted.

"Alice, is that a crossbow? What the heck!" Kathy asked, looking between her wife and daughter.

"I just hauled it out to–" she began, but Emily interrupted her.

"You already had this? I never saw it before."

"That's because you've been a little kid for a long time, and Mom asked that I keep my toys out of sight from nosy buggers like you," Alice told her, trying to alleviate the tense moment she found herself in.

"But why are you working on it?" Emily asked. The rag and the oil were obviously used to shine it up.

"I was just looking at it," Alice fibbed, glancing at Kathy, who didn't buy it either, but Kathy realized they needed to divert the teen's attention. "You have to take care of your things."

"Speaking of which, did you make your bed? Didn't you say there was an end-of-year pep rally you wanted Sean to take you to?" Kathy put in.

"Oh, yeah," the teen said, sounding suddenly excited. As she left the office, Em looked over her shoulder, her long hair swinging. and said, "I want to try that thing!"

Both moms waited until they heard her bedroom door close before Kathy turned on her wife. "Are you insane?!"

"I thought she had already left for the pep rally. I thought it was safe to start working on it." Alice raised her hands in mock defense against her wife's attack.

"Where in the world did you have that hidden?"

Alice just raised an eyebrow. "I think it's time we took the battle to them, don't you?" she asked instead.

"Were you at the house in the valley?" Kathy asked, wondering when she would have gone there. She'd only just brought the Land Rover home and hadn't gone anywhere except to dinner with the family.

"No, I haven't been there in a long time. Although, I should probably…" she mused, thinking of her previous uses for that house.

"Sell it," Kathy finished for her.

"What?"

"Yeah, I think it's time you sold that place as well as the Malibu house."

"Well, the Malibu place, sure. But the house in the valley? Where would I train?"

"How about here?" her wife gestured towards the exercise room their daughter used just as much as their muscle-bound son.

"Oh, and where do I hide the knives when I'm not using them?" Alice asked, sounding a little sarcastic.

"Well, I–" Kathy began and realized it was futile. She knew about the house and the reason for it. It wouldn't do to bring those types of things into this house.

"Look, I haven't been there in a long time. I haven't worked out like that in just as long," she gestured to her booted foot. She had the cane nearby in case she needed it for balance, but she liked that she could still

drive her new Land Rover without worrying about the boot. She needed to get out. She had *things* to do.

"So, what is this?" Kathy asked, getting back to the crossbow.

"I thought I'd use that sedan for target practice," she said with a small grin twitching at her lips.

Kathy laughed. She didn't object. She was sick of that car sitting outside their gates too. "Can I come?"

Alice was surprised. She had planned to hobble out to the cliffs and come at the car from a different angle, so they wouldn't know the attack was coming from the Weaver estate. "I only have the one crossbow," she pointed out, picking it up and giving it a rub with the rag.

"Show me how it works. I want some payback after all we've endured."

Alice gladly showed Kathy how it worked. This reminded her of when she helped Kathy get over her hurt all those years ago. Teaching her how to work with knives and how to physically defend herself had given her self-confidence. They went out into the backyard, far from the eyes of their intended victims and away from the children.

"I like this," Kathy admitted as Alice showed her how to put her foot in the cocking stirrup. The crossbow was planted firmly on the ground, so she could pull the string back. Alice had to use her left foot since her right foot was booted, but the challenge was something she was clearly up to.

"These are cocking ropes. They make it easier for women to cock a crossbow since they don't always have as much upper body strength as guys," Alice said, showing her the correct way to use it. She put the middle of the cocking rope in the groove. It tightened the rope as she pulled on it. "You put the bowstring on the groove, and that creates the tension that pulls the bowstring back." She demonstrated. "Some people

mark the spot with a marker, so they put the hooks in the same spot every time. You want the hooks oriented correctly." She showed her wife that the open side of the hook was facing outward.

"Jeez, I thought you just pulled it back, put the arrow in, and let it fly," Kathy murmured, trying to remember everything Alice was showing her. Neither of them noticed that Emily was watching from one of the upstairs' windows. With the window ajar, she was listening unashamedly as Alice instructed her mother.

"You want to adjust the ropes slightly, so the handles are aligned with each other and you have even tension on both sides. That way, you are pulling them at the same time. You don't want to be inconsistent here as it will affect your accuracy and make it harder to pull the bowstring back."

It was obvious Alice had done this before, and Kathy watched as her wife effortlessly pulled the string back in one forceful, fluid motion. They both heard three clicks. "Now, it's cocked and in the ready position," Alice showed her. "Keep your finger off the trigger and the safety on." She demonstrated the process for Kathy, then had her repeat it.

"Now, the arrows?" Kathy asked, getting a little excited by the instruction and Alice's proximity. Her breathing was coming a little faster.

"They are called bolts since they are shorter. Only put one bolt in the groove. See the colored fletching or "wings" at the end? You want to make sure that is placed in the barrel groove. You could damage the bow if the bolt isn't placed correctly. You also have to ensure the nock at the very end of the bolt is positioned against the bowstring correctly." Alice demonstrated, keeping her hand behind the safety line, which she pointed out to Kathy, and sliding the bolt into the barrel until it was firmly seated.

"This bow has a clip," she pointed, "that keeps the bolt from sliding around."

"Now, are we ready to fire?" Kathy asked excitedly.

Alice nodded and looked around for a target. They had elephant palms in the gardens, and the leaves would be perfect.

Kathy's first shot totally missed, and the bolt sailed above the concrete of the pool and landed in the water.

"Take a more athletic stance. Since we don't want to be seen, aim down the scope, or these sights here," she showed her wife the notched V in the stock.

"Why'd I miss? That's a pretty big palm."

"You jerked the trigger when you fired and that decreased the accuracy. Keep the crossbow aimed at your intended target."

"Are you going to kill those men with this?" she asked, only slightly horrified at the thought as she lowered her voice.

"No, but their tires and their pretty paint job may suffer some damage," Alice answered, outraged. Besides, with the boot on her foot, there was only so much she *could* do.

They practiced a while, losing bolt after bolt in the pool, but Alice didn't mind. She could retrieve those. After a few more shots, she put bowstring wax on the crossbow strings. "That will keep the strings from breaking," she informed her fascinated wife.

"Can't we practice without the arrow?"

"No, you should never fire a crossbow without a bolt in the latch. That could ruin your weapon. The vibrations, also known as the kinetic energy, is absorbed by the bow. You can also be hurt by that," she explained patiently to Kathy.

The elephant palms weren't thick enough for the bolt and wouldn't absorb the blow, so Alice hadn't planned on practicing. "Okay, get the kids going, and when they've left, we can use this for real," she promised as she put the crossbow down by the pool and began to take off her boot.

"What are you doing?" Kathy asked, confused.

"I'm going to retrieve those," she gestured to the bolts lying at the bottom of their pool, "and put different points on the tips. I don't want them traceable to us."

Kathy smiled as she left to get the kids ready. By the time she returned, Alice was nowhere to be found, and she was disappointed, thinking her wife might have gone without her. Finally, she found her in their bedroom. She was laying out clothes for Kathy to wear. Alice had already changed and slicked her hair back, and she was wearing a black knit cap.

"These look like jogging clothes," she commented as she started to change. God, she was already tired, and she had merely practiced for a short time with the bow.

"Yes, they are," Alice agreed as she finished dressing. "That way, if anyone sees us, they will think we are out for a jog. Although," she gestured to her boot, "they won't buy that I'm doing anything more than a fast walk," she chuckled.

Kathy was always impressed by how carefully Alice thought things out. She knew her wife probably wasn't overjoyed to have her along, but Kathy had hated how she always felt excluded. She heard the Velcro tightening on the boot as Alice stood up. "Do you need your cane?" she gestured to the walking boot she was wearing.

"Probably, but I'm going to wing it," Alice responded.

They walked to their back gate. Kathy had the gate key firmly in hand, and they went through to the path that ran along the tops of these bluffs

down to the beach below. Instead of taking that path, they continued past their own property towards some of their neighbors'. Walking briskly, Alice held the crossbow down at her side, so it was less visible. Kathy was carrying a dozen bolts in her gloved hand. Alice had been sure to rub them down, so no fingerprints could be used to identify them.

They approached the sitting car, the two men inside reading the news on their phones. Alice knew the light from the phones would temporarily blind them in the night, but she also knew the darkness of the night would make accuracy with the crossbow more difficult. She didn't think Kathy would hit anything but gave her the first shot. She watched as her wife confidently used the instructions she had just received to pull the bowstring back and insert a bolt. She aimed carefully at the tire they intended to flatten, instead hitting the rear quarter panel squarely. Both men sat up, wondering about the noise, but before they could move to inspect, Alice had another bolt in the crossbow and was aiming. This one didn't land where she wanted it either. She was out of practice, but she did manage to hit the tire, although it landed on the opposite side of the car from where she had planned. At least it hadn't hit the metal cover. The tire air blew out as soon as the sharp point of the bolt pierced it.

"More?" Kathy asked, excited and exhilarated at this unexpected caper.

"I don't know if we have the time," Alice said as Kathy prepared to put another bolt in the bow. Alice was watching the men, and she was shocked when one got out of the car just as Kathy fired again. This bolt hit the steering wheel column.

"Jeezus!" they both heard the man yell as he dove for the asphalt.

"I think we should be going now," Alice whispered, trying not to laugh at her exuberant wife. She'd enjoyed this far too much.

They backed away, the dark clothes making it easy to fade into the night as they headed for the path behind their house. It was much more dangerous traveling at this time of night, and they stayed near the fences, so they didn't get too close to the bluff's edge.

"Think they will leave?" Kathy asked as she unlocked their gate and they passed through.

"No, but I'm sure they'll think twice before screwing with us anymore," Alice answered. She hadn't intended to hit them, but damn, Kathy had come close with that third shot.

Alice hid the crossbow under her desk, using clips to keep it where no one would find it. She dropped the extra bolts into the bottom drawer, forgetting about the incident in the rush of data she had to analyze. Kathy watched as her wife became engrossed in the various drawings of buildings and structures, wondering which properties those were. Kathy busied herself reading the information Alice had given her about Carmen, and she was growing increasingly angry with the girl as she realized how manipulative she had been with their daughter.

* * * * *

The excitement of the evening didn't end immediately. Kathy was still worked up hours later when they finally went to bed after the kids got home. She shared a tub with Alice, who was enjoying the freedom of taking a bath without her boot. This led to a pleasant moment in the tub, each achieving a satisfactory outcome of the lovemaking that ensued, but that wasn't enough for Kathy this time! As Alice dried off, put her boot back on, and grabbed her robe, Kathy vigorously pushed her against the wall of the bedroom.

"Wha–?" she began, but Kathy was kissing her hard.

"That was so exciting…" Kathy murmured between the hot kisses she was pressing on her surprised wife.

Alice wasn't used to Kathy being this forceful. Their love life had kind of sucked in the past few months, but this was exciting! She went to push back, but Kathy wasn't having any of it.

The brunette pushed against her wife, holding her firmly in place as she kissed her deeply, her hands running along Alice's bath-warmed body. The heat between them was no longer caused by the hot bathwater but from the blood running below the surface as Kathy began kissing along her neck. She was sucking the skin into her mouth and tonguing her. Slowly, she kissed her way down to Alice's breasts, kissing intensely on each tip.

Alice gasped. Her breasts used to be so pert but now hung down. It also didn't help that there was excess flesh on them, but Kathy didn't mind, and the sensations still pulsed through her wife's body as she tongued the nipples, sucking on them and causing Alice to gasp again. Alice plunged her hands into Kathy's hair, urgently pressing her wife's mouth against her bosom.

Kathy's hand moved between Alice's legs, searching for and finding the erect little nub she knew would be waiting for her. At first, she wasn't sure if Alice was still wet from the tub or from her own juices, but she debated that only momentary when Alice responded to her attack. Kathy kissed her way across Alice's stomach and down until she could toy with the nub using her tongue and lips.

Alice looked down at her wife kneeling between her legs. The sight of her wife's mouth busily engaged on her clit caused Alice to throw her head back and bang it against the wall. She didn't mind the pain. Her brain was short circuiting as she came quickly against Kathy's mouth. The orgasm

in the tub was adequate but *this* was primal and all-encompassing. She felt marvelous as she bucked against Kathy's mouth.

Kathy smiled, thrilled that she could still cause this response in Alice after all their years together. The heel of her hand rubbed against the flesh causing pleasure-pain that she knew her wife enjoyed. She began to rise and kiss her way up her wife's body again, reaching around to squeeze Alice's firm buttocks.

Alice, completely aroused and satisfied with her own orgasm, grabbed her wife's robe and spun them, nearly falling over the boot on her leg as she attempted to take control of the situation and give her wife the same treatment she had received. It took longer as Alice didn't have the agility she'd once had, but Kathy was biting down on the back of her fist to hide the cries of her own orgasm as Alice slowly stood up and continued to play with her heated body. As she played once again with Kathy's breasts, a frown appeared on her face.

"What? You don't like them anymore?" Kathy teased as her eyes started to focus. She was enjoying the aftermath of the passionate lovemaking with her wife.

"No, that's not it. You have a lump," Alice said as she tenderly felt it.

"Oh, that. It's nothing. I have another one over here," she said, pointing to her other breast. "It's just a fatty lump."

"When is the last time you had a mammogram?" Alice asked.

"C'mon, don't ruin the moment with–."

"I'm serious. When is the last time you went for a checkup? Between the kids and me, when have you taken time to care for you?"

Kathy stood transfixed. What a helluva comedown after a thoroughly enjoyable lovemaking session with her wife. She fixed her robe, pulling it

closed to her wife's gaze as she shrugged her shoulder. "I don't really remember," she admitted.

"Will you make an appointment…Please?" Alice added gently.

"Okay, okay. I'll go. Jeez," she said begrudgingly.

"Thank you," Alice replied, attacking Kathy again with her lips. She wasn't finished. Their time together had been too pleasurable to allow it to end on a discussion about healthcare. With Kathy's legs wrapped around Alice's waist, the women soon forgot about the lumps and enjoyed each other in a healthier way.

* * * * *

"Can I come with you?" Kathy asked a few nights later.

"Come with me where?" Alice hedged, not used to talking about these things.

"Alice, does that belong to the guy that caused our IRS problems or one of the guys that robbed us?" she gestured to the diagrams of the properties.

"Jeez, is it that obvious what I'm doing?" Alice asked aloud, wondering if the children had noticed too.

"No, but I know you, and I also know *that* is going to slow you down," she pointed to the boot on Alice's leg and foot. "I want to help. What he did affected my family too," she said earnestly.

Alice didn't have the heart to turn her down. They had to be careful though. Emily was getting too good about sneaking around and overhearing things. They planned their strategy carefully.

"Want to go hear a motivational speaker?" Alice asked a few days later, holding up a paper she had just printed out.

"Why would I want to hear a motivational speaker?" Kathy asked, wondering if that was simply a rhetorical question. As she looked at the paperwork, she realized Alice was talking about going to see the former Senator Ken Edwards. "Are you going to kill him?" she asked, lowering her voice.

Alice laughed. "No, but he is going to wish he was dead. That's who is watching our house," she gestured to the car outside. The car they shot up had been replaced with another car, and she smiled thinking about using it for target practice again.

"What are you smiling about?" Kathy asked, her own lips parting as she returned the smile.

"Wanna go target practicin' tonight?" Alice asked, reaching to unlock the desk and check on the bolts she'd hidden there. Her smile faded when she realized they were gone. "What the hell?!"

"What's the matter, babe?"

"Look! That's where I put them," she indicated the empty drawer. "Or did I?" she mused as she began to open the other drawers one by one. None of them contained the missing bolts. Next, she got down on her hands and knees to check for the bow, and it was missing too. "What the hell?!" she repeated as she started to rise and hit her head on the desk. "Christ!" she swore as she rubbed her head and pulled it out from under.

"Are you okay?" Kathy asked worriedly. She had heard the head hitting the wood, and it sounded painful. Alice rarely swore, but she knew it was probably justified by that hit.

"The bow is missing," she informed her wife.

"What? Who...?" she asked, and they both spoke in unison, "Emily!" Kathy looked angry as she walked to the doorway of the office and called up the stairs, "Emily, will you come down here please?"

Alice finished pulling herself out from under the desk and sat on the chair, still rubbing her head as she listened to their daughter galumphing down the stairs. "Yes, Mom?" she called before she came down the second set of stairs.

"Could you come down here please?" Kathy asked, revealing nothing in her tone.

Alice had to hand it to her wife. She would have gone up to the kid's room and confronted her, but this was a much better to way to handle things. She was still rubbing her head when the teen walked into the office, looking curiously at her parents.

"Did you take something from this office?" Kathy asked carefully, looking at her daughter. She was as tall as Kathy now.

"Take something?" she asked, trying to sound innocent.

"Did you take the crossbow from under the desk and the bolts from the drawer?" Alice asked more directly, looking angrily at the teen. Damn, her head hurt! She stopped rubbing it to glare at her daughter.

"I just wanted to try it…and then…" she began, shifting uncomfortably as both her mothers looked at her. Now, she looked decidedly guilty.

"And then?" Alice prompted. She wasn't feeling very patient at that moment.

"I…ah…used it."

"Oh, my gawd! Emily, did you kill someone?" Kathy gasped, and both Emily and Alice looked at her in horror.

"NO!" Em nearly shouted. "I just used all the arrows up."

"Bolts," Alice corrected automatically. "Were you target practicing?" she asked, relieved Emily hadn't killed anyone. That hadn't been *her* first thought, and she wondered at where Kathy's mind had gone for that one

"Sorta," the teen said uncomfortably. She was squirming. "I just wanted to teach them a lesson."

"Teach *who* a lesson?" Kathy asked, her tone angry. She wanted to get to the bottom of this *right now*.

Emily looked up, first glancing at Alice then at Kathy. She had meant to have the bow back under the desk before they found out. She couldn't retrieve the arrows, and she had thought maybe they wouldn't notice. Apparently, she was wrong.

"What aren't you telling us?" Alice put in.

"Do I have to–?"

"Every word," Alice commanded, waiting. She knew she wasn't going to like her daughter's answer, and she could see Kathy was becoming impatient.

"I shot out the Pasternacks' windows," she said, looking down at her shoes and mumbling.

"You did *WHAT*?!" Kathy asked, practically shouting. She hoped she hadn't heard correctly.

"I shot out the Pasternacks' windows," she repeated, a little louder.

Alice nearly laughed. Instead, she asked, "Did you break all nine of their windows?"

The teen looked up, and Kathy looked at Alice with a frown. "There were nine bolts left," she reminded her wife.

Emily shook her head. "No, I didn't hit all the windows at first, but eventually, I did."

"Eventually?"

"Well, I retrieved the arrows that hit the stucco," she explained.

Alice restrained the laugh that wanted to spill out. "Were they home?"

Emily shook her head again.

"Where's the bow?" Kathy asked at the same moment Alice asked. "They are going to find your fingerprints, you know?"

"No, they aren't. I wore gloves," Emily explained, then looking at Kathy, she said, "The crossbow is in the garage. I was waiting until you were gone, so I could put it back," she gestured at the desk.

"How did you know to wear gloves?" Alice asked, turning the teen's attention back on her.

"I watched when you were showing Mom," she gestured to Kathy. "I listened to everything you told her."

Alice sighed, wiping her hands across her face. "You realize—" she began, then changed her mind as another thought occurred to her. "When did you do this?"

"Earlier tonight," the teen replied in a small voice as she fidgeted, wondering how much trouble she was in.

"You could have been caught!" Kathy gasped.

"They weren't home. I saw through a fake account that they were going out to dinner. I already had the bow, and I practiced like you did," she told Kathy. "I went over there and started firing at the windows. I missed several times but retrieved the arrows, so I could try again."

"Don't they have a security system?" Alice asked, thinking this through and wondering if they were going to have to hire Portia to defend their daughter. This was serious.

She nodded but added, "I turned it off."

"Turned it off how?" Kathy asked, sounding incredulous at their daughter's story.

"I knew the code. They hadn't changed it, so I turned it off and shot the windows. That took a while since I had to keep retrieving the arrows

until I could hit the windows. Then, I turned it back on with a delay and left."

"No one saw you?" Alice asked.

The teen shook her head.

"Do you know how dangerous that was?" Kathy asked angrily. "You could have been caught!"

"I know, but they need to pay for–"

"Emily, you know it was wrong. That bow is not a toy, and you were told not to touch it," Alice told her.

"But I–"

"Nothing you say right now is going to justify using that crossbow to get even with the Pasternack family," Alice interrupted.

Emily hung her head and then, they all heard the gate buzzer. Alice looked up at her computer and switched it to their security system. She saw a sheriff's car at the gate. She glanced at Kathy, who was frowning at her. Alice nodded her head towards the screen, and Kathy walked across the room to look at the camera shots. Emily followed and gasped, "They know!"

"No, you don't know that. You are to stay down here," Alice said, rising, then with one quick swipe on the keyboard, she cleared the screens. She used her cane to move over to the panel on the wall where another camera showed her the face of the person who had buzzed. "Yes?" she called into the speaker as she pressed a button.

"Hello. We are doing a routine patrol and would like to ask you some questions, if we may?" the officer said, looking earnestly into the camera.

Alice pressed another button, opening the gate to the patrol car. Looking at her daughter, she repeated, "You stay down here and don't move." She limped out of the office and Kathy hurried to catch up with

her. By the time the sheriffs got to the door, Alice had made it up the steps and was opening it. "Hello. Can I help you?" she asked innocently. "Hi there, ma'am," he said, removing his hat and looking curiously from Alice to Kathy.

Alice could tell this officer didn't know the problems they had experienced last year; he didn't know them. "Good evening. Would you like to come in?"

"No, ma'am, that won't be necessary. Do you know your neighbors?" he asked, gesturing to the estates on either side of their own.

"Mmm, a little but only in passing really," she admitted. "What is this about?"

"One of your neighbors was vandalized and we," he indicated the other officer down a few feet on the steps, who was watching them and looking about, "are inquiring if any of their neighbors saw anything."

"Vandalized? What happened?" Alice asked, sounding as if butter wouldn't melt in her mouth.

"Oh, a few windows broken. Have you had any problems like that?"

Alice shook her head and glanced at Kathy, who repeated the gesture. "We had a break-in last December but nothing since," she told him and saw the other officer nod. So, he had known about that. "Don't they have cameras or a security system?"

"Apparently, none of that was working at the time," he admitted. "Well, ma'am, if you see anything, please give us a call."

"We'll do that," Alice assured him, and as he went to leave, she asked, "Um, which neighbors were vandalized?"

"Oh, the Pasternacks over there," he said, pointing to the house across the acres.

Alice nodded and watched as they went down the stairs. She waited until they were through the gate and in their car before she shut the front door and leaned against it. She looked at Kathy and rolled her eyes. They both headed towards the stairs.

"Why did you ask who it was?" Emily asked, proving she had been listening.

Alice waited until they were all sitting on the couch before she said, "Because most people would be curious who it was, and if I hadn't asked it might have raised their suspicions."

Emily swallowed this bit of news.

"Now, young lady, we need to talk about this," Kathy put in.

"They are going to get away with–" the teen began defensively, but Alice cut her off.

"No, we got a huge settlement out of them."

"That's nothing. They won't even miss the money, and money won't get back my…" she trailed off.

"No, it won't, but I'm dealing with it, and you have to trust me on that." Alice warned her, "No more of this, Emily. I won't countenance you destroying property like that. You might have been caught, and you can bet they are going to be suspicious of you. We live far too close for them not to think of you or your brother for this act. Do you want Sean to get in trouble for something he had nothing to do with?"

Emily shook her head, suddenly scared that her big brother was going to get into trouble because of her. He'd already been threatened with suspension from school for fighting. She hadn't meant for that to happen, and she didn't want to get him in trouble; she just wanted to scare them a little. She thought the cute little arrows would work perfectly for that.

"Go get me the bow, and your mother and I will discuss your punishment," Alice said sternly.

Emily got up from the couch and dejectedly went to fetch the bow where she had hidden it in the garage.

"What are we going to do?" Kathy asked in a whisper.

"I have no idea. What's the usual punishment for using a crossbow on someone's windows?"

"Don't make me laugh," Kathy said, putting her hand up to her mouth to hide her smile. She could see Alice was having trouble keeping a straight face as well.

Emily came in holding the bow and handed it to Alice. She looked dejected. Alice hobbled over to the desk to place the bow on it.

"Look, honey, we just want to keep you safe. Trust me. These people will pay for their crimes–" Alice began.

"They wrote a check, that's it! And Carmen isn't paying," she argued passionately.

"No, but in the long run, what do you want to see happen to her? Do you want her dead?"

"Nooo," Emily moaned, horrified at the thought as she sat on the couch, "but I want her to pay for what she did."

"She will, honey, but it is going to take time. I want you to promise you won't do anything again without discussing it with me first," Alice directed, and when Emily looked like she would argue further, Alice put up her hand. "No! Promise me."

"I promise," the teen mumbled, hanging her head.

"Now, your mother and I haven't agreed on a punishment yet. I don't want you to tell anyone about this. I mean no one, *ever*! You never know who might be listening, and you certainly cannot ever tell anyone in an

instant message, text, or any form of written word. No bragging and no confiding in even your dearest friends…Okay?"

Emily looked up, troubled.

"You haven't already told anyone, have you?" Alice asked, concerned.

She shook her head solemnly, and her mothers believed her.

"She will suffer. One day, she will suffer. I promise you!"

"Will I get to see her suffer?"

"You want revenge that bad?" Alice asked kindly.

"What she did–"

"Was horrible," Alice finished for her. "But do you want revenge so bad that you are willing to see her hurt?"

Emily had to admit that she didn't want revenge that badly.

"What *do* you want?" Kathy asked kindly, feeling badly for her daughter and everything she had gone through.

"I don't know," the teen said, despondent and starting to tear up. Kathy put her arm around her daughter's shoulders, turning her head aside to cough into her sleeve.

Alice looked at Kathy and wondered about the cough. She hadn't sounded congested earlier. "What would you like me to do?" she asked the teen sadly.

"I don't know, Mom. I just feel so helpless. They got away with everything, and Carmen is still able to move about freely, doing whatever she wants, whenever she wants, without any repercussions."

"She couldn't go back to your old school. She and the others were expelled," Kathy reminded her.

"Yeah, but she talks about how great her new school is, and–"

"Don't listen to her. I bet if you stopped checking up on her and making fake accounts to see what she is up to, you wouldn't feel like this,"

Alice pointed out. "She also didn't get into any schools here on the peninsula. Not even the private schools would take her or the others, and her parents have to drive her into LA to go to school."

"How do you know?" Emily asked, looking up, her eyes filled with tears. Kathy looked up too, wondering.

"Let's just say I made sure of that," Alice told them with a small eye roll to express her fake innocence. That gesture had them all smiling slightly. "I didn't do anything any other concerned parent wouldn't have done. Who wants deviants in their local school system?" she asked in her most prissy voice. They all laughed out loud at that.

"That's funny," Emily admitted, wondering how Alice had accomplished that. "But they still haven't paid for what they did—"

"No, and they may never pay for it," Alice admitted ruefully. "All we can do is move on and live well. People like that eventually get theirs. You have to believe in fate."

Long after their daughter had gone to bed, Alice and Kathy lay in bed talking about the events of that night. Emily knew she was going to be punished for her actions, just not that night. "You know, you can make sure those people pay for what they did," Kathy pointed out.

"Yes," Alice nodded as she agreed with her wife. "And, they will. In time, they will."

"What do you have planned?"

"Nothing yet," she admitted. "Again, everything in time."

* * * * *

"We are watching the former senator. Ken Edwards is a natural target, and if Alice Weaver goes for him, we've got her," one of the FBI agents reported to Director Wolf.

"It isn't going to work," Madelyn told her boss. "She is smarter than that."

"We'll see," he replied. "She's bought tickets to his latest session for her and her wife."

"A session?" Madelyn asked, raising an eyebrow as the agent left the room after giving them a report on his latest findings.

"Yes, one of those motivational talks he gives where he sells the books and other paraphernalia that earn him a good living. He," his chin indicated the agent who had just left, "told me that Alice bought two tickets to the next event."

"How closely are you watching this Ken Edwards?"

"Well, he is out of prison, so we can have others watch him for us," he admitted, not giving her a complete answer.

Madelyn understood they wouldn't tell her everything, but she felt that setting up Alice Weaver was a bad idea. They still didn't have the information they needed from her. She sighed. They weren't going to listen to her. What did she know?

* * * * *

Ken Edwards' voice tapered off as the spotlight moved, and he was finally able to see his audience. He swore he was seeing a ghost from his past. He realized he was seeing an older version of Constance Weaver in the form of her twin sister, Alice. Sitting next to Alice was a pretty brunette. He recognized her as the wife from the surveillance photos.

What a perversion! During the time he had been in prison, they had passed laws allowing LGBT people to marry. As a senator, he would have completely opposed such legislation, even if he had participated in such perversions in prison. He justified his behavior in many ways, not the least rehabilitated from his crimes. Had anyone explained to the asshole that these were not perversions but his own sanctimonious beliefs, he would not have understood.

Returning to his well-prepared speech, he continued to inspire those that were new in his audience as well as those who already believed in him. He still had his good looks, if slightly aged, and people were drawn to that as well as his charismatic charm, which would have won him the White House had he been able to continue in politics with his wife at his side. They had been presented as the perfect couple. Unfortunately, they had participated in auto-erotic asphyxiation and had killed too many people. Constance Weaver was one of their victims. Connie, as she was known to Alice, had been a bit of a wild woman. As time went on, her husbands had increased her wealth, each leaving her marginally richer than the last. But when Connie had happened upon the Edwards, she had, unfortunately, met her match. After Ken had filmed the accidental killing of his own wife, that film and many others had found their way into the hands of multiple TV stations across the country. Time and the public's short attention span made the Edwards' story old news. People had forgotten his many crimes.

"Alice, it's a pleasure to see you again," was his phony comment when he saw her at the meet and greet afterwards. He had been signing books when he saw the two women walking by and got up to greet them.

Alice would have been content had they simply not run into the man. She had seen him falter when he first saw her in the audience and that was

enough for her…for now. She knew she unnerved him. She didn't say a word, just stared at him with her odd cat-like eyes.

"And this must be Kathy. How do you do?" he asked, offering her his hand.

Kathy ignored it, looking him up and down and wondering what rock he had crawled out from under. His good looks had faded, and she could see his blonde hair was thinning. She turned to cough into her arm, and it turned into a spasm, which she hadn't anticipated. Alice looked at her, deeply worried.

The former senator also looked at the woman in alarm and hurried on, pretending they hadn't noticed him or his attempts at a greeting.

"Are you okay?" Alice asked her.

"Water," she gasped, and they headed for a drinking fountain where she calmed her cough. "That was so weird," she stated.

"Kathy, have you made that appointment for a checkup yet?" Alice asked, taking her arm and leading her out of the conference room. Not surprisingly, Edwards had not been very motivational to either of the women. Truthfully, they found him quite boring.

"No, but I will," she promised as they stepped outside into the southern California sunshine. Both reached for their sunglasses.

"Mrs. Weaver?" a voice stopped them as they began to descend the steps of the hotel.

"Yes?" they both answered, looked at each other, and laughed.

"Mr. Edwards would like to talk to you," the man gestured. Judging by the dark glasses and earpiece he was wearing, he was obviously security.

"Well, we don't wish to talk to *him*," Alice emphasized, dismissing the man and attempting to walk past him, her hand on Kathy's arm.

"I don't think you understand," began the man, grabbing Alice's arm.

Alice had anticipated the move and swung her outstretched arm around his quickly, twisting it behind him and using her booted leg to step down on his insole and then kick him in the shin. "You let me go!" she said loudly and distinctly, so that passersby saw her as he went down. "How dare you touch me! Are you aware that Edwards man is a killer? He killed my sister!" Her voice got louder and louder, and people were obviously listening since they were staring at the man she had downed. A crowd began to gather.

"Alice," Kathy gasped, pulling her away. She wasn't sure if Alice was playing with the man or had lost her cool. They walked in silence. Alice limped on her booted leg, using Kathy as the crutch she hadn't thought to bring. Her cane was in the SUV. Once they were in the Land Rover, Kathy asked, "Are you okay?"

"Oh, yes. My public display is going to bother him," she said cheerfully, pointing behind them with her thumb as she started up the SUV and put on her seat belt. "Want to unnerve someone else today?" she asked.

"What in the world?" Kathy asked, grinning at the cheerful tone in Alice's response. "What do you have in mind?"

"Let's strike a blow for us and for Emily," she said mysteriously as she headed for Beverly Hills. The Land Rover was gobbling up the miles effortlessly as she drove. They talked about everything but where they were going and what they would do. Kathy was enjoying the time with her wife, and she loved the mischievous tone of Alice's antics.

Kathy looked on curiously at the beautiful homes they passed. They had looked at some of these very estates when they were in the market for a home because Alice had wanted something near the ocean. She'd been

very certain what she wanted, and she hadn't like it when they moved from the marina because they'd outgrown that condo.

Alice stopped at a large gate and pushed the button, waiting for the tinny voice to ask her, "How can I help you?"

"Alice Weaver to see Artum," she said and waited.

"See *who*?" the voice came back almost immediately, responding too quickly to feign innocence.

"Tell Artum I know he is living here. This was Sebastian's house, and I know he took it over. If he doesn't see me now, he will regret it."

Kathy recognized the name Sebastian; she had met him at Alice's memorial service. He had been a big, bluff man, a Russian, and she looked curiously through the iron gate which opened shortly after Alice's statement. She glanced at Alice and saw she was grinning as she drove onto the estate. The circular drive ended in front of the big mansion. Kathy was alarmed to see men with automatic weapons walking about. As Alice parked the Rover, one of them came towards the SUV and opened the door for Kathy. Another jerked Alice's door open, and she was amused when they indicated she should get out, then immediately began to pat her down.

"I suggest you take your hand off my boob before I break your arm," Alice said conversationally, prompting sounds of outrage from Kathy. In two seconds flat, the man in front of Alice went down, his gun in her hand and held against his cheekbone. Dropping the gun, Alice sprinted as fast as she could move with her brace, heading around the front of the vehicle to see Kathy protesting violently about being patted down by another guy. "Hey! That's my wife you're manhandling," she protested. The man turned to her, his gun crossing in front of his body. Alice grabbed it and

heaved it upwards where it hit his chin, and the man went down, surprising them both.

"Easy there," a voice called with amusement as Artum came out onto the porch of the mansion. The scene before him reminded him of a conversation he'd had with Sebastian on this very porch:

"Don't touch Alice Weaver," Sebastian rasped, reaching imploringly towards Artum. They were sitting in the evening air and Sebastian, who was on oxygen, had a tube fitted around his face, so it could go up his nose.

"Who is this Alice Weaver?" Artum asked, wondering how she had the impunity to come and go despite all their security precautions.

In his mind, Sebastian thought about Alice, going over the many years he had known the woman. Artum thought he had fallen asleep when he finally opened his mouth to speak. Breathing heavily, he had difficulty getting the words out. "I...do...not...know...really." Over the next hour, he slowly and methodically explained what he did know about the mysterious woman. He spoke of how she had bested him time and again, and he had learned not to cross her. He reminisced about how he had lusted after her and had been unequivocally rejected. Before exhaustion took him, he grabbed Artum's arm and implored him one more time, "Don't touch Alice Weaver. She...will...kill...you...all."

Artum wasn't alarmed by the warning, but he took it to heart. There were many people in their organization throughout the world who were not to be touched. Their immunity allowed them to enrich all without restriction, but this was unprecedented since Alice wasn't part of their organization, at least not from what he could tell. He nodded in agreement as Sebastian fell asleep. Alice Weaver would not be touched.

Now, remembering that long-ago day when his uncle had warned him about Alice, he still could not see why Sebastian felt the warning was necessary. He glanced curiously at his man, who was slowly rising and saw the mayhem on his face caused by the blow that had downed him. As he brought his gun to bear, Artum called, "I wouldn't," in Russian.

Alice looked up at the two men on the porch and recognized Artum. She straightened her clothing and looked to make sure Kathy was okay. She nodded curtly after seeing the look on her wife's face and straightened her own clothes that had been mussed by the man putting his hands on her.

"Artum," Alice said coldly. "I come to pay a visit, and this is how you greet me?"

"You should have called first," he said with a grin. She didn't seem that formidable an enemy, and yet, even from fifteen feet away, those eyes were making him uncomfortable. She was wearing a boot that he'd seen on people after they broke their leg, and she was limping. She was a petite woman with spikey, blonde hair. What was it about this woman that had so unnerved his uncle? "Would you like to come in?" he invited, his hands gesturing towards the mansion.

"We would," she stated, taking Kathy's arm at the elbow with her fingertips. "Let me introduce my wife, Kathy."

"How do you do, Mrs. Weaver?" he asked charmingly, taking her hand when she was close enough and kissing the back of it while he bowed at the waist. He stood again and released her hand, a twinkle in his eye as he looked at her. "This way please," he gestured towards the house again where the door was being held open by yet another man. He noticed his other guard had gotten up from the ground on the other side of the Rover, and he glared at them both, earning a slammed door on each side of the Rover. *These guards of mine!* he thought.

"May I offer you a drink?" he asked as he welcomed them into his living room and made his way to a bar in the corner. The room was excellently appointed with couches, rich woods surrounding the windows, beautiful display cabinets, and a large mantle over the fireplace. "Would you like to sit down?"

It was the mantle that drew Kathy's attention, and she stopped to look at something, drawing Alice's attention to it with her eyes. After this exchange, they went to sit down.

"Thank you, but a drink isn't necessary," Alice answered for them both, making sure that Kathy was comfortable and exchanging another look with her. "I've come to you because I have a problem you can help with me with."

"Oh?" he asked, pouring himself two fingers of whiskey in a glass. "What could I possibly do for you?"

"You can tell me where I might find a man who works for you. His name is Iggy?"

"Iggy?" he asked, as though he had never heard the name.

"Come now, Artum. Let's not play games. Ignat Koslov works for you, and I would like to speak with him about a situation he and his men caused my wife and me." She sat back on the couch, seemingly unconcerned. Kathy looked on curiously, realizing there were meanings within meanings in what Alice was saying. She never noticed Alice's sleight of hand as she dropped something into the couch.

"A situation?" he asked, sounding intrigued as he came to sit across from the two women on the couch.

"Oh, yes. He has caused you a bit of embarrassment, I believe?" she asked, sounding cordial as she leaned forward slightly, her fingertips touching the edge of the coffee table briefly before she leaned back again.

Kathy looked from Alice to the man sitting across from them. He was tall and handsome, and he looked dangerous. His beard was trimmed immaculately and sculpted along his jaw. His jaw was twitching. Alice could see she had hit home with the word 'embarrassment.'

"What kind of embarrassment are we talking here?" he hedged, hoping it hadn't become public knowledge. His tone of voice had changed slightly.

"I think you may not be aware of this particular embarrassment?" she put in, a smirk on her face.

"How would I know what you are talking about?" he inquired, becoming impatient with her cryptic statements.

"If you knew what he had done, you wouldn't have my Fabergé egg displayed on your mantel over there," she said, nodding towards the beautiful cobalt blue and gold specimen. "I would like to talk with Iggy *personally*," she emphasized.

"I'm sorry, I don't know what you mean…" he began, but he was afraid he did know. Iggy had given him the egg as a sign of respect, apologizing for taking so long to pay his dues. He had thought the man had finally realized he owed great homage to the new leader.

"I see. You are going to protect him then?" she asked conversationally, studying her fingernails as she looked up suddenly, peering across them and right in Artum's dark eyes.

"No, I'm not protecting him. I simply don't know what or who you are talking about. I don't know anyone by that name."

"You, sir, are a very bad liar. Ignat Koslov violated my home. He came onto my property, broke down my front door, and stole that item," she nodded towards the egg, "as well as many other valuable items. I can get you a list," she said sarcastically. She continued when he would have

interrupted, "However, I can see there is no honor in this house anymore. He touched my daughter, and he and his men threatened to put her in a whorehouse, discussing quite intimately how she would be used," she told him, watching Kathy from the corner of her eye.

Kathy sat up straighter. She was outraged that Alice hadn't told her that!

"As I see you will defend your employee, I must warn you now...Turn him over to me and return my things, if you want this to all be over."

"I'm sorry, I don't know what you are talking about," he said, but he was disturbed to realize he believed her. How dare she come into his home and threaten him...It was a threat, wasn't it? She'd stated her conditions but not really in a threatening manner.

"I'm sorry too," she said and looked at a horrified Kathy. "Shall we go?"

Kathy nodded numbly as Alice helped her to her feet. Artum immediately rose, showing he had some manners.

"I am sorry for any misunderstanding between us–" he began diplomatically, but Alice interrupted him, raising her hand to halt his insincere apology.

"There is no misunderstanding," she clarified as she escorted her wife from the room with the taller man following. Alice made sure Kathy was tucked in the Rover. "Say nothing now," she warned her quietly. Alice limped around the SUV, smiling—smirking really—at the two men she had downed. One was going to have a black eye and the other still had blood on his lip. She got behind the wheel of the Rover and started it up, driving slowly down the circular drive and waiting a heart-stopping moment for the gate to open, fearing it might not and ready to ram it if

necessary. Slowly, it opened, and she glanced in the rear-view mirror to see Artum staring thoughtfully after them from the porch.

"Why didn't you tell me what those men had said about Emily? How did you know–?" Kathy started up as soon as they turned down the road from the driveway.

"Because I didn't want you getting angry about it and chewing on it until I could do something," she told her wife honestly, glancing over as she pulled her seatbelt tighter. "We are going to do something," she continued, "I promise." "Right now, let's go meet with Charlotte and get that house on the market."

Kathy blinked at the abrupt change of subject. She'd been horrified and angry, and now, she was confused. "Which house?"

"The one in Malibu. Have you changed your mind?" she teased.

"How can you do that?" Kathy marveled, calming down.

"What? Sell a house?"

"No, how can you make a complete about-face during a conversation?"

"About-face about what?"

"Stop playing games with me, Alice."

Alice chuckled. "I'm already over being mad. You just found out what they said, so you can be angry. You will deal with the anger in your own time. Meanwhile, I wanted to get a lot accomplished today and tonight, and I know you have been wanting me to put the Malibu house on the market for a while. I want you to go to the doctor...so it's a tradeoff. Okay?" Alice reasoned.

Kathy shook her head, sighed loudly, and said, "Okay, deal."

Alice chuckled again as she drove to Charlotte's office. She was surprised and pleased to find the realtor was in. The woman was ecstatic to take that listing again. She didn't promise anything, but Alice gladly

gave her the keys to the place, signed the paperwork, and agreed to have professional pictures taken. She didn't understand why they couldn't use the previous pictures since the place had been off the market for less than a year. It wasn't like it had changed a lot.

"We should have Sean go over and get the computer games," Alice mentioned to Kathy as she drove back towards Palos Verdes and home.

"I'm surprised he hasn't mentioned those games," Kathy put in. She was so tired. They'd done so much today and that news about what the men had said about her daughter was preying on her mind. She was glad Emily hadn't realized what those men were saying. She was already frightened enough.

"Well, most of the games are duplicates," Alice reminded her, keeping an eye on the traffic and noticing the car that had just started following them again. She hadn't seen the tail while she was in Beverly Hills, but it had followed them to the hotel where Ken Edwards had given his pretty, little motivational speech.

"Tell me, Alice. What was the point of today's visit to Artum?" Kathy asked.

"You have to ask?" Alice was amused. It had been quite a full day, and she'd like to go out tonight but didn't know if Kathy was up to it. She looked tired and worn out.

"Why don't you give me a recap?" Kathy requested. "I'd like to know what you are thinking."

"Well, we unnerved Ken Edwards. His people are going to be given a chewing out. He doesn't suffer fools gladly and thinks of those who work for him as minions and peons. They are paid to do a job, they are not paid to think. So, if they don't do the job, they will earn his ire. I'm betting he's having a royal hissy fit at someone today because no one warned him

we would be coming. He would have expected someone to give him a heads-up that we would be in his audience.

"Just now, I wanted to serve warning to Artum. I'm sorry I didn't tell you some of it beforehand, but I wanted him to see your honest reaction. I didn't want anything to look feigned about you playing the outraged mama. I believe your shocked reaction worked in our favor, and when we go after his assets, he is going to want to give me Iggy on a silver platter." She paused to grin at Kathy, "Believe me, we are going to destroy a lot of his assets in retribution."

"And the house in Malibu?"

"Well, that was to make up for not telling you what those men said about our daughter. It's a peace offering. I checked the other day, and the prices in Malibu are sky high right now. Maybe it's because summer is almost here, but in any event, I don't expect the house to be on the market for very long. It was a good investment, and since the government will be looking at our tax returns pretty closely for the rest of our lives, this should look good."

"What about your girlfriend?" Kathy asked suddenly. She had been meaning to ask her about the other woman for a while. It was one of those things that she wanted to bring up but wasn't sure she wanted to know the answer since Alice was once again in her bed.

"Girlfriend?" Alice asked, genuinely confused.

"I saw the nightgown on your bedroom floor when you showed me the house."

Alice started to laugh. then seeing Kathy's outraged face, she sobered up before saying, "That was a plant."

"A plant?"

"For whoever was watching the house. I wanted them to think I had someone there. I wanted them to worry a little if they checked the house and found it there, wondering how she had gotten in there without them seeing. I left that lying there for days. I cannot tell you how hard it was for me to not clean it up," she admitted.

Kathy started to laugh. She knew how fastidious Alice was, and yes, it would have been extremely hard for her to leave a piece of clothing lying on the floor.

"It was just a bonus that you came over when you did and saw it."

Remembering the reason for that visit, Kathy sobered. "Did you ever look into Linda's death?"

Alice glanced over and saw the sadness on her wife's face. "Did you love her that much?"

Kathy immediately shook her head. "No. I did think of having a future with her at one time, and I'm just sad that she is dead."

Alice was relieved. She hadn't wanted to tell Kathy, but she decided there was no time like the present. "I think Ken Edwards had Linda killed."

"What?"

Alice nodded. "I think he was hoping to pin it on me along with the IRS cloud and the other investigations. He never thought I'd go to the CIA and get a letter exonerating me from prosecution. I am betting he doesn't know why all investigations stopped and he's still wondering why we aren't destitute and homeless."

"How are you going to pay him back? Are you going to kill him?" Kathy might understand Alice's reasoning if she wanted to kill him. The man certainly deserved to die if he had ordered Linda's death, not to

mention everything he had put them through. Still, she didn't have to like it.

"Oh, no. I'm thinking we should let him live," Alice told her as she turned onto their street.

"What? Why? What do you have up your sleeve?"

"I think allowing him to live will be more of a punishment than simply killing him. Killing him would end his suffering too quickly. I honestly haven't thought about him in years, which is why it took me so long to figure this out. Now that I know who's behind this, more pieces of the puzzle are starting to fit together. He isn't alone in this. I believe he's called in some old favors, and I'm just trying to figure out exactly how many people are involved. I want to see who the players are in this mess he has made."

Alice's eyes narrowed as she approached their driveway. The gate was open, and a car was parked at the bottom of the walkway. She didn't hit the garage door opener as she approached like usual. Instead, she parked in front of one of the garages. They both got out of their car and looked at the man, who had gotten out of his car when they drove up.

"Can I help you?" Alice asked, walking around to the passenger side of their car and standing next to Kathy.

"Are you Alice and Kathy Weaver?" he asked.

Feeling a premonition of imminent disaster, Alice took one step forward, putting Kathy behind her and putting herself in a position to protect her wife. She said, "Yes, we are. Can I help you?"

"You can drop the fucking lawsuit against my daughter!" he told her, walking forward belligerently.

"Careful, Mom. That's Angelica's father," Emily called from the top of the stairs where she had just come out with Sean.

Angelica. That was one of the three girls who had shared Emily's pictures online. Alice remembered seeing this man at the school. He had been the one who refused to cooperate. The parents of the third girl had willingly turned their daughter's phone over to the police, and it proved she not only took the pictures but was sharing them.

"You don't know who the fuck you're dealing with," he got right up in Alice's face, looming over her petite frame.

"You don't know who you are dealing with either," she answered, a tight little grin forming on her face.

He almost took an involuntary step back when he noticed her odd-colored eyes. It angered him that she had caused him to show this sign of weakness, almost as though she could scare him.

"I suggest you leave. You are trespassing." She cocked her head sideways slightly, daring him to touch her or assault her.

"I thought you could be reasoned with…" he began belligerently.

"You thought wrong. That's what lawyers are for."

"You're going to beggar me with–"

"Considering what your daughter did, maybe you should be beggars," she taunted, waiting to see what he would do. Her stance made her appear ready to take him on, despite the brace on her leg. Kathy knew it, and Emily recognized it from her videos, but the man had no clue. Sean was worried about his mothers. He had pressed the panic button when the man slipped through their gate and had come banging on their front door, so he knew security was on the way. Neither of the kids was going to open the door to that.

"Why don't you just leave?" Sean asked from where he stood above them on the steps. "Security and police are already on their way."

"That's it! You rich folks just hide behind your fences and the law," he spat out, looking at the young man, then down at Alice again. He was trying to intimidate her with his size. As he looked at Kathy, Alice stiffened. She heard Kathy discreetly coughing behind her.

"Yeah, that's us, hiding in plain sight," she said mockingly. "Why don't you take my son's advice and leave before you find yourself in a whole heap of *more* trouble." The man's back was to the security vehicle she could see coming down the road. Its lights were flashing, and it was followed closely by a sheriff's vehicle. "Breeding shows. Your daughter probably did what she did because she has a father like you."

Kathy gasped from behind Alice at her taunt. Emily's eyes opened wider, and Sean was certain he was going to have to leap to his mother's defense. He took a couple involuntary steps down the stairs to get within range, just in case. If anything, at least he could tackle the big guy.

"Who the fuck do you think you are–?!" he began, but Alice cut him off.

"I'm the homeowner, and you're trespassing," she said loudly as the security car pulled up with its windows open. "You weren't invited here, and you're threatening me."

"Mrs. Weaver, is everything okay?" one of the officers called as the security guards exited their vehicle.

"No, I'm not okay. This asshole has been threatening me, and he is trespassing on private property. I've asked him to leave a couple times."

"Sir, you are going to have to leave, or we will arrest you for trespassing," one of the officers began.

"No, you arrest him for trespassing *now!*" Alice directed them, seeing the sheriff getting out of his patrol car. The way the sheriff and security vehicles were parked, this guy wasn't going anywhere.

It took an hour before they finally took Angelica's father away in handcuffs. Despite his arguments, they towed his truck and charges would be filed. Alice got her way. She agreed to stop at the sheriff's substation to sign the paperwork for her complaint in the morning. No matter who the guy was, he would be spending the night in jail.

"Jeez, Mom. I thought that guy was going to take a swing at you," Sean said after they had all gone.

"How the hell did he get in?" Alice asked, glancing at Kathy as they all started walking up the stairs to the front door.

"I'd just gotten here with the RAV, and when I went inside the doorbell rang. I thought that was odd since I hadn't heard anyone at the gate. He must have driven in right behind me, and as I walked through the garage, I didn't see him."

"Aren't you supposed to ask before you use the RAV?"

"I did ask. Mom said I could use it," he gestured to Kathy, who nodded.

Alice shook her head. Just what she needed, another situation. Later, she commented to Kathy, "See, I don't go looking for these things, they find me."

"I know," she answered, coughing again. "You are a drama magnet."

"Are you calling the doctor tomorrow for an appointment?" Alice fretted.

"Yes, I promise. Weren't we going out tonight?" Kathy inquired. "Didn't you have something planned?"

"Damn! I forgot, and with all this drama, we might be too late," she answered, looking at the time on her phone. "Think the kids will miss us if we have a date night?"

"A date night?"

Alice nodded. "That's what we are telling them. Make sure you change into your black jogging outfit while I go pack the SUV. Could you bring my clothes with you?"

* * * * *

Artum learned of the fire from the Los Angeles Fire Department the next day. They showed up at his gate accompanied by the police and informed him that a warehouse he owned had gone up in flames the night before. Apparently, it was a six-alarm fire and had burned so hot there was nothing left. The police wanted to know if he had any enemies since it looked like the arsonists had used some type of accelerant. Artum cursed after they filled him in on all the details. He had lapsed his insurance on that warehouse thinking no one knew he owned it, so it was an unnecessary expense. After Alice and Kathy Weaver's visit the previous day, he hadn't been very pleased, and he was certain now, he should have heeded Sebastian's warning. Over the following nights, he lost two more warehouses and a house that no one even knew he owned. Two of Iggy's subordinates were missing as well. At first, he questioned if Alice Weaver might be behind his losses, but he sincerely doubted it after meeting her and seeing her physical stature. Somewhere, he must have created an enemy, and it was costing him a lot! "Where is Iggy?" he asked after learning about the fourth fire.

* * * * *

Kathy hadn't been this excited or scared in a long time. They'd gone to the house in the valley and taken their time to lose the tail. Alice had gone

to a panel in the 1970s wall, which Kathy had never noticed before. She lifted the wood paneling, and behind it were standard wall braces with multiple shelves of supplies between them. Kathy watched, amazed, as Alice picked and chose from the array at her fingertips. Once her arms were full, Kathy helped her pack everything in the SUV. Later, they hauled everything into that first warehouse but not before they stopped to fill a couple gas cans and pick up some throw-away cell phones. Alice had expertly picked the lock of the warehouse, and the two women hauled in the gasoline, spilling it along the aisles from one shelving unit to another. When they were ready, Alice showed Kathy how to wire a cell phone to a primer cord.

"When I call this phone," Alice indicated one of the throw-away phones she had purchased, "it will send a spark to this," she pointed at the cord, "and the spark will trigger that," her arm gestured towards the gasoline that ran deep into the old warehouse.

"Why are there no guards?" Kathy wondered, rubbing her gloved hand across her nose and noticing the smell of gasoline on it.

"Artum must not think it is necessary, and it's probably cheaper," she reasoned as she rigged the set-up, left the phone on the desk, and rose. "Let's get out of here," she said as she glanced around for cameras one more time before they left the warehouse.

As they were driving away, Kathy asked, "When will you trigger it?"

"Let's get a couple more miles away and then call," she said, reaching into her pocket for the paper where she had jotted down the number of the phone left on the desk. "Would you like to do the honors?"

Kathy eagerly reached for the phone and after turning on the overhead light, she keyed the number into the phone. "When do I hit send?" she asked eagerly.

"Are you that eager to commit a felony?" Alice asked, amused as Kathy turned out the light.

Kathy coughed to hide her laugh. "No, but I do want to meet this Iggy guy and have a few words with him on our daughter's behalf."

Alice nodded. She was quiet as she drove a while longer, then she said, "Call the number."

Kathy eagerly pushed the send button. She heard the phone ring once, then a second ring, and finally, it made an unusually fast beeping sound. "That's it?" she asked, disappointed as she closed the cheap flip phone.

Alice nodded. "We don't want to be anywhere near that warehouse when it goes up in flames. Watch the news for the video."

"That's anticlimactic," Kathy said, her voice sounding a bit down.

"I have a police scanner, if you want to listen to that," Alice pointed out.

They went out several nights in a row and were enjoying the excitement of hitting what seemed like random places, first some warehouses and then, a good-looking, empty home. One night while they were at one of the businesses, they ran into two of Iggy's friends. They recognized them as two of the men who raided their home, despite the disguises they had worn. Alice's research had produced photos of the men, and once she verified their identity, Alice let Kathy have a few words with them.

"We did nothing, missus," one of them denied, his thick accent revealing his fear. Alice had tied the men up with wire, and it was now digging into his wrists. If either of them struggled too much, the wire was positioned to cut into their veins.

"Ty izhesh," Alice said in Russian, repeating it in English for Kathy's sake, "You lie."

He looked surprised by the petite blonde with the slicked back hair. Her accent was rough, but he understood her clearly, even before she repeated it in English.

Kathy looked surprised. She hadn't heard Alice speak Russian before. It was obvious both men understood her, judging by their shocked expressions.

Kathy told them in no uncertain terms what she thought of them and their comments about their intended plans for her daughter.

Alice asked a couple pertinent questions, but it was obvious they were reluctant to answer. She pulled a knife from her metal belt to help convince them, and after she began to slice along the neck of one man, he began to spill the information she required. The other man needed no further encouragement, and he too began giving her relevant information. They didn't tell her anything she hadn't already learned on her own, but they confirmed and verified things for her.

"Now, what do we do with them?" Kathy asked in a whisper as Alice covered their mouths with duct tape, wrapping it completely around their heads. Alice had explained if they only wrapped their mouths, the duct tape might come off when it got wet from the saliva. Kathy appreciated the new knowledge. She would have laughed at the trivia, if they weren't in such a dire situation.

"What do you want me to do with them?" Alice asked. She kept her voice equally low where they stood across the room, her eyes glittering in anticipation.

"What do you mean, what do I want *you* to do with them? I'm in on this too, aren't I?"

"Okay. It was *our* daughter they talked about," and Alice went on to remind Kathy exactly what the men had talked about doing to Emily. Kathy's ire rose even higher.

"I'll kill them!" she vowed.

"Killing them won't make them suffer," Alice pointed out.

"If we let them go—"

"They will warn the others," Alice finished for her.

"Then, what?"

"If there are no bodies, the police can't investigate. If no one ever finds them, they will always wonder what happened to them," she pointed out. "If we don't kill them, we won't have their deaths on our conscience…but they will die, and they will suffer," she added.

"So…what? We leave them here?" But Kathy realized if they burned this place down, there would be bodies. "No, not here," she shook her head. "Then where?"

Kathy helped Alice put the tied and taped men in the back of her SUV on top of some plastic she had draped there. She tied their legs together and warned them, "Ne dvigaysya." They would have fought, but she'd knocked them down, stunned them, and the wire on their wrists hurt. Her admonishment, "Don't move," would be obeyed…for now.

As Alice drove to Long Beach, Kathy sat in silence. Her heart was pounding, and as badly as she wanted to discuss their plan, she would obey Alice, who had touched a finger to her mouth to shush her. The radio muffled any sounds of the road and any sounds the men might make as they surreptitiously attempted to free themselves from their bonds. Once off road, Alice exited the car in order to cut the chains off a gate. Once through the gate, the Rover bounced over the ruts of the road, its headlights illuminating oil derricks. Kathy looked at Alice in alarm and

wondered where they were and why they were here. Alice was looking for something, and when she found it, she turned the vehicle around, backed it up a ways, then braked and turned everything off. Kathy followed Alice to the back of the Rover when she finally got out.

"Okay, get out!" Alice told the first man, cutting the ties on his feet, so he could walk. "Ladno ubiraysya," she repeated her command in Russian. "You stay there," Alice pointed with her knife at the other terrified man, the one whose legs were still tied together. "Ty ostan'sya tam," she added in Russian for effect, proving to everyone that she knew the language, albeit imperfectly. Alice had examined the ties and saw where the wire had cut into the men's arms causing them to bleed. She couldn't see any blood in her SUV, but she knew that didn't mean a thing. She was concerned about leaving DNA evidence behind, which was why she also examined the plastic to see if either had gotten off it. She closed the back of the Rover, leaving the second man inside as she led the first man towards one of the derricks. Before Kathy could ask where they were going, Alice threw out her arm to stop her wife from taking another step forward. The man was not so lucky. He hadn't seen Alice stop Kathy and kept walking forward where he fell, quite abruptly, disappearing from sight. They heard a splash, but it was far away and muffled. They only heard because it was dark, and the sound carried.

"Whaaa–?!" she began, but Alice grabbed her again and pulled her back before she fell in another hole.

"Be careful! This place is full of holes, and if you aren't vigilant, you could fall in too," Alice told her.

"Did he just fall in an oil hole?"

"Sorta. It's probably more like a maintenance hole. They are all over the place, and they are never checked. Most are covered, but this one

wasn't and probably hasn't been for years. We were closer than I thought," Alice admitted. "It's been years since I was out here. I thought they would have covered it up by now."

"Have you used this method to dispose of enemies before?" Kathy asked, and when Alice didn't answer, she had her answer. Alice hadn't told her much about her past kills, and she really didn't want to know more. Together, they returned to the SUV and got the second guy out of the Rover, heading back towards the hole. He struggled, worried when they returned so quickly without his partner. Alice smacked him repeatedly, unsettling his equilibrium when she struck his ears. Despite the wires cutting into his arms, he had thought to fight her, but all thoughts of fighting vanished as he went down on his knees. Alice drove her booted foot into his spine and sent him headlong into the hole. Both women turned away, so they didn't hear him hit bottom. Alice pulled the plastic from the back of her SUV, rolled it into a tight ball, and flung it into the hole after the men. The smell of oil was strong around them, and the mighty derricks were endlessly pumping, coaxing the life blood of this area to rise and make some company rich.

They both got back in the Rover, and Alice started the engine and drove away. She stopped just long enough to close the gates behind her and place the chain around the posts with her gloved hands, so it wouldn't arouse suspicion. They were strangely silent on the ride home, both seemingly enjoying the music. As they turned down their street, they saw their watchers' car, only tonight, one of the men was on the side of the road, back about ten feet in the weeds, peeing. Alice turned her Rover, aiming straight for him. Her headlights clearly highlighted his body as he dove out of her way. They both laughed at his discomfort as Alice expertly pulled the Rover around the waiting car and into their driveway.

She peeled her gloves off before stuffing them beneath her seat. Kathy followed suit, still chuckling.

* * * * *

Alice finally got to remove her brace on the same day Kathy went in for a full checkup. Kathy hadn't used a doctor in years, so she didn't know this general practitioner. Dr. Lenoir was quite thorough and ordered further tests after asking several pertinent questions and listening to Kathy's lungs. A mammogram and x-rays would make Kathy's life very interesting over the coming week.

Alice was busy. She and Kathy had been to several of Artum's properties in the past few nights while setting things up. She'd had to search far and wide to obtain everything she needed and avoid arousing suspicion. Her shopping list was rather…eclectic, you might say. She parked the Rover in city parking and boarded a train going downtown. Their watchers were either too lazy to follow or didn't have direct instructions to follow her on foot, so they had no idea where she went on the train or what she carried in the boxes and bags she brought back. Some of the packages couldn't be seen since she wore a backpack to keep her hands free in case she needed to act quickly. Downtown Los Angeles was not the best neighborhood, even in the light of day.

So far, they hadn't had to openly kill anyone, but she knew it was only a matter of time. She didn't count the two in the hole in Long Beach. She was certain they had either died during their fall or would eventually die of starvation in the hole, and she didn't care which. But she realized their disappearances might have some in the organization rethinking their choices. Her nights were filled with plans and shaking the men that Ken

Edwards had assigned to follow her had proven difficult. Either his instructions had changed, or these were a better caliber of watchers.

Her plans had to be put on hold temporarily when Kathy began her tests. Alice's days were now filled with concern about Kathy as she waited with her for the mammogram results, x-rays, and other tests Dr. Lenoir ordered.

"She must think there is something wrong if she's ordering all these tests," Alice worried.

"Well, I haven't been checked out in years, and I think she's just being thorough." Kathy dismissed Alice's concerns, but she was worried too. Dr. Lenoir had poked and prodded and some of it had hurt.

"Mrs. Weaver, please come in with your wife," the nurse suggested from where she stood in the doorway. Alice would have come in anyway, but she stood immediately, pleased she didn't have to balance on the brace anymore. Her leg felt thinner and much lighter without the cast and brace. It also felt weaker, so she was being cautious; her gait was still a bit awkward.

"What do you think she wants to tell us?" Kathy whispered. "Maybe I'm pregnant?"

"Lucy, you've got some 'splainin' to do!" Alice said in her best Desi Arnaz impression. "Could you imagine…at our age?"

"Our baby is nearly grown up," Kathy admitted with a smile, remembering Emily as a baby. She had filled out so much in the last year, and it was good to see. Kathy looked at Alice with a critical eye too. She had also filled in a little this past year, and it looked good on her.

"Mrs. Weaver? Kathy?" the doctor came in, closing a folder she had been reading. She shook both their hands. "I'm glad you could come in. I have your test results here," she said as she took a seat. The nurse sat

down in front of a computer on the other side of the small examination room and waited. "I need to run some biopsies, but this," she pulled an x-ray from the folder, "needs to be looked at by another doctor." She held the x-ray up to the light for a quick glance, then put it on the lightboard on the wall and flipped a switch to illuminate it for all to see.

Both Alice and Kathy were shocked. The x-ray showed several spots across Kathy's chest. In fact, it showed many, many various sized spots.

"Is something wrong with your tests?" Kathy asked, looking at the odd x-ray.

"No," the doctor responded firmly.

"Is it cancer?" Alice asked.

"We don't know yet. We need to run more tests."

"What in the world? How did they get like that?" Kathy asked. She had felt the mass that Alice discovered in her breast, and she knew there was another in her other breast. Now, she could clearly see both those masses on the x-ray, but there were numerous others of various sizes. They almost looked like pencil-sized dots all over the x-ray. Did she have measles?

"These are inconsistent, and I want to biopsy this one," she said, pointing to the mass in the right breast. "That will allow us to draw it out and get an idea what we are dealing with. I also want to do a full body scan since these," she pointed to spots that were visible at various points above her skeleton on the x-ray, "also don't make sense."

"So, what is it? Breast cancer?" Alice asked, trying to bore holes in the x-ray with her eyes.

"That's just it, we don't know. These spots are too erratic, too random. They aren't behaving like normal cancer cells or masses."

"So, lymphoma?" Kathy asked in a small voice, feeling ill at what she was seeing.

Again, the doctor shook her head. "I don't know, and I want you to see one of our oncologists as soon as possible. The pattern is too random, and it doesn't seem to be targeting one specific system. This is too spread out too. Something…" she murmured, thinking aloud as she looked at the x-ray again. "Have you been working with asbestos? Maybe you were refitting a house and inhaled something?"

Kathy immediately shook her head. "No, we haven't done anything like that." She didn't count the warehouses they had visited in the past few nights because she hadn't inhaled any of the smoke they caused, but she had certainly coughed a lot from the activities they were involved in.

The doctor questioned her extensively about her travels and any other activities that might have caused what they were seeing on the x-ray. She asked about foods she might have eaten, all kinds of arbitrary questions, but both Kathy and Alice could see she was grasping at straws. She was attempting to find the cause of these erratic growths that didn't exactly look like cancer cells. Kathy agreed to undergo the fine needle aspiration biopsy procedure. Alice held her hand as she watched the needle being inserted into her wife's breast. The doctor pulled it out after she hit the mass she wanted to aspirate. Alice could tell it hurt Kathy because her hand tightened. but even more painful were the thoughts playing on her mind about what this could mean.

"How long until you get the results of that?" Kathy asked, pointing at the needle the doctor had labeled.

"A few days," she admitted, looking sadly at Kathy. "Can you come in tomorrow for the full body scan, so we can see if that tells us anything about what we are dealing with?" Dr. Lenoir made it seem quite urgent,

and both Alice and Kathy were reeling, but they agreed to come back the next day. They were mute during the drive home in the Rover. Alice reached out and held Kathy's shaking hand.

"I'm going to lose my hair," Kathy said.

"I could shave my head again in solidarity," Alice said, trying to lighten the mood…and failing.

"Oh, my God. I never thought about cancer," Kathy said quietly, starting to cry.

Alice pulled over to the side of the road and parked, pulling Kathy into her arms while she sobbed. It was a long time before she stopped, and Alice's shoulder was completely soaked with her tears. Just as Kathy began to breathe normally, they heard a knock on the passenger side window And saw a Los Angeles policeman was standing next to the car. Kathy sniffed, and Alice handed her a tissue before she rolled down the window.

"Can I help you, officer?" Alice inquired politely.

"Is everything okay, ma'am?" he asked, looking at the two women closely.

"My wife just learned some devastating news, and I was comforting her," she told him honestly. She hoped he wouldn't give her a ticket or hassle her; she wasn't in the mood.

"Ah, I see," he said, noting Kathy's puffy eyes and seeing her dabbing at her nose with the tissue. "Please be careful when you get back on the road," he said as he gave a mock salute and backed off, returning to his vehicle.

"Well, he was nice," Kathy said in a raspy voice. She was obviously still quite upset.

"We weren't doing anything wrong," Alice pointed out.

"For a change," Kathy added, and they both chuckled. "How are we going to tell the kids?"

"Do you want to tell them before we know the results of the tests? You know, this is going to scare them."

Remembering how many times they had been scared by their other mother's faux deaths, Kathy decided to wait and tell them when they knew what they were dealing with.

* * * * *

"If you don't want to go out this time, we can wait," Alice offered when she saw how upset Kathy was feeling that evening. The kids sensed something was up with their parents but didn't want to ask. At the same time, they were both pleased with how often their parents had gone on date nights, or so they thought.

"You know, I really want to go out and destroy something," Kathy admitted eagerly.

Alice smiled slightly. These trips to the properties Artum owned under various pseudonyms to hide his assets were becoming routine. They'd destroyed several buildings now, and he couldn't possibly have traced it to them…yet.

"Okay, but this should be the last one," Alice stated with a gleam in her eye. Kathy laughed. She knew this might be just the beginning of the war. She realized that Alice had planned the invasion of Sebastian's old warehouses with military precision. Alice didn't do anything halfway. She had been calculating, thorough, and given the amount of time she'd held back due to her broken leg, she had been very, *very* patient.

"Maybe we should rethink this location," Alice stated when she saw this warehouse had guards.

"Do you have an alternate warehouse on your list?" Kathy asked, wondering if their night out was ruined. She needed something to get the tests and their possible results out of her head. She coughed slightly, feeling defeated.

Not wishing to disappoint Kathy, Alice leaned back in the SUV and began to fill their packs with the supplies they would need. Each of them carried a gas can that had been blackened, so no one could see the telltale red color of the plastic containers. Alice had thought about getting jerrycans for the SUV, so no one would question why she was carrying so much gas if she got stopped, but this was not the time to think about accessories for her Rover. She'd parked down the street and hoped no one jacked the expensive SUV. She thought about getting another vehicle for this kind of trip and was reminded of the vehicles she had sold from the storage units.

They waited for the security guard to pass before sneaking into the warehouse. Alice went one way and Kathy the other, both splashing gasoline on the floor and onto the boxes on the shelves. They had no idea what was in the boxes, but they could guess. Leaving the gas cans in the shadows by the foot of the stairs, they climbed together to a loft-like section of the warehouse where the offices were located, ducking down to avoid being seen. Alice began to wire the office with detonation cord. Kathy had seen that the highly explosive core of the cord was wrapped in a reinforced, drab olive-gray plastic coating. Alice explained this would transmit a detonating wave, which was perfect for their efforts.

As Alice wired the cord to a throw-away phone—one of several she and Kathy had purchased at random gas stations—Kathy wandered to the

desk, keeping low and away from the windows that surrounded the office. Just as Alice finished her work, Kathy hissed, "Alice, look at this!"

Alice crept next to her wife, watching that her head didn't rise above the windows where they might be seen by the guards in the warehouse below. She looked at the accounting books Kathy had found, her eyes opening wide in shock at the various amounts and names she saw listed there. She glanced at Kathy, who nodded to confirm she had seen correctly.

"What are you doing in here?" a man's voice asked gruffly. Both Kathy and Alice turned towards the door where Richard Pasternack stood.

He recognized them instantly. Alice ran to shut him up, but it was too late. He yelled, and the nearest security guard was already running up the steps. Alice wrestled with Richard, and he was shocked that she would attack him. This worked in her favor, and she was able to stun him by striking his head against the frame of the door. He went down when she struck him a second time, using his head as a bouncy ball. By then, the security guard had arrived and was trying to cuff Alice. He grabbed her wrist, but she twisted away. Alice adroitly grabbed the cuffs from his hands, wrapped them through her fingers, and used them as brass knuckles, slugging him in the jaw and shocking him with the ferocity of her attack. He couldn't believe this petite woman could best him, but he went down when she kicked him in the head and knocked him out.

"Help me," Alice ordered Kathy as she shut the office door. Kathy wheeled the office chair over and helped her wife pull a stunned Richard up onto it.

"He...isn't...very...light...is...he?" Kathy huffed and puffed.

Alice grinned as she cuffed Richard to the chair with the security guard's cuffs, then found a second pair for the other wrist. When they were done, they wheeled him back to the desk.

Alice hog-tied the security officer with his own tie and dragged him further into the office. She hoped the commotion hadn't attracted anyone else's attention. So far, it seemed quiet down in the warehouse.

"Do you want to explain this, *Dick*?" Alice asked Richard when he was able to focus. Seeing Alice and Kathy Weaver standing before him in black outfits, he realized they must be the ones that had started the fires at Artum's warehouses and house!

"I'm not telling you jack." he asserted stoutly, then swallowed reflexively when Alice pulled a hunting knife from the sheath on her leg down by her ankle. It matched her outfit perfectly, and he hadn't noticed it earlier. She held the blade to his neck.

"Do you know what it feels like to bleed to death?" she asked him in a quiet voice while gesturing to the ledgers. "You might want to explain who these companies are…quickly!" she threatened. She could hear people moving around in the warehouse below, so she kept her voice low. She knew that Richard's silhouette could be seen through the frosted glass of some of the windows. She made sure he wasn't visible from the clear windows intended to allow anyone in the office to look out over the vast warehouse, rolling him to the side of the desk away from those windows. She knew the people below would expect to see one shadow, not two or three. She gestured to Kathy to stay low. "Go through the drawers," she whispered to her wife.

Kathy, her heart pumping wildly at this turn of events, obeyed instantly. Her eyes bugged out at the cash that spilled from the drawers when she opened them. "Look at this!" she hissed to Alice, trying to

contain the excitement in her voice as she showed her wife the bundles of used bills. Then, she came across bundles of bills in larger denominations that had been shrink-wrapped. They looked brand new, and she wondered if they were real.

Alice tilted her head and said, "You better start talking, *Dick*," letting him decide if she was referring to his name or a certain body part.

"I am not telling you–" he began, and Alice turned her knife without hesitation, plunging it through his hand secured to the chair. His body jerked automatically, but the handcuff around his wrist kept him in the chair. Anticipating his scream, she clamped her other hand over his mouth, and that was when she smelled gasoline and realized the scent must be coming from her glove.

Kathy's eyes almost bugged out of her head when she saw her wife stab their neighbor. She quickly turned back to the desk drawers, opening them one at a time and placing the cash she found on top of the desk.

"Richard…Dick…you got something you want to say to me before I kill you for refusing to say jack?" Alice asked conversationally. She pulled the knife from his hand, watching his eyes flare as she stabbed the knife faster and faster into the wood of the chair between his fingers.

Richard had never been so frightened in his life. Sandi told him she had seen Alice Weaver at Sebastian's, but he hadn't believed her. He had refused to go along with his wife's plans, even after Carmen had gotten in trouble at school. He was disappointed he hadn't been able to buy the Weaver estate from bankruptcy, but there were other properties. They already owned several they had acquired through various deals. Working with Sebastian, and now, his heir Artum, had proven quite lucrative. The pain in his hand was excruciating, but the smell of gasoline had him worrying about what they might have done with gasoline in the warehouse.

Alice's normally polite demeanor was nowhere to be seen. Who was this person before him? Her eyes were frightening. He nodded to let her know he did have something to say to her, and as soon as she removed her glove from his mouth, he began explaining about the companies and people in the ledgers before him.

Kathy was aghast! He spilled information for quite a while. Alice just studied him to ascertain if he was telling the truth. She was also listening in case any of the security guards came to see where their co-worker had gone. When the guy on the floor started making groaning noises, she stuffed crumpled papers in his mouth to shut him up. When that hadn't worked, and Richard had faltered in his recitation, she kicked the guy in the head again, silencing him. She gestured for Richard to continue, and after that display, he sped up.

"Wait, so they manufacture some of the chemicals here in *this* building?" Alice interrupted to ask.

Richard nodded, hoping if he kept talking, it would buy him time, and someone would come and rescue him from the predicament he found himself in. He thought of screaming but knew that was a bad idea. The look in Alice's eyes told him she'd silence him permanently before she was done.

"Is that all you have for us?" Alice finally asked when he seemed to run out of steam.

He nodded reluctantly. They had gone through most of the pages of the ledger before him.

"Kathy, put that and that," Alice nodded towards the various ledgers, "in your pack. Leave the cash; we don't need it."

"But Alice…" Kathy began. She knew there were hundreds of thousands of dollars on the desk now.

"We don't need it!" Alice stressed. "There is blood on that money plus cocaine and other drugs," she told her wife, who pulled the ledgers out carefully with the tips of her fingers once she realized what they were dealing with. When they heard a slight noise near the door, both Kathy and Alice looked up and were horrified to see Emily opening the door slowly, her eyes wide at the sight before her.

What Emily saw was her mothers wearing black outfits. Alice was holding a knife at the ready, and Kathy was stuffing a ledger into a bag. There was a strange man hog-tied on the floor before her, and Carmen's father, Richard, was handcuffed to a chair in front of a desk filled with cash.

"Emily!" Kathy gasped, seemingly frozen in time.

"What in the world are you doing here?" Alice asked, shutting Richard's gaping mouth with her glove before he could say anything.

"I snuck into the back of the SUV and hid under that lap blanket you carry," Em confessed, her eyes wide.

"Quiet!" Alice hissed, hearing what she thought was movement in the warehouse below. They all froze. Kathy and Alice exchanged looks, and Emily continued to take in the scene before her. She was shocked! She'd heard Alice's story about Kazakhstan but seeing her at work with Kathy helping her was beyond anything she could have imagined.

"How long have you been in here?" Kathy whispered, frozen in place next to the desk where she had finished packing up the ledgers they were taking.

"I saw you two go up the stairs and waited to follow. When they didn't return," she gestured at the security guard and Richard Pasternack, her eyes flaring as he recognized her, "I worried that you might need help."

Kathy and Alice exchanged looks. There was nothing they could do now since Emily had seen what they were up to. Alice slowly released Richard's mouth with a hissed warning, "Be quiet or else..." She didn't need to finish her sentence. They both knew what 'or else' meant. She looked around the office, nudging Kathy as she picked up another bag she'd found. "I had another thought," she told Kathy and began stuffing money into the bag.

"I can tell you where there is even more money," Richard began, trying to bargain for his life. He proceeded to tell the two women a fount of additional information as they listened. Alice shoved a cleaning rag she had found lying about the office into his mouth when she realized he was finished. Emily's eyes looked like they were going to bug out of her head as she watched. "Shhh," Alice said, touching her fingers to her lips. She'd heard something from below. It was probably one of the other guards. She gestured to Kathy that they should go, realizing they'd been there far too long.

"What about the phone?" Kathy asked, gesturing to the wire that lay unconnected.

"Too late. We don't have time," Alice answered as she handed Kathy the bulging bag of cash after swinging the pack over her shoulder.

"Mmm hmm," Richard tried to speak around the rag. His hands gripped the chair as he struggled, but Alice ignored him. He was no longer important, and she had to get her family out of here.

She grabbed Emily by the arm, touching her finger to her lips to signal the teen to be quiet.

They eased the office door open, but instead of going down the same stairs they had used to come up, they went farther along the corridor. Slowly, they opened other office doors until they found another stairwell,

which they climbed down cautiously. Alice was worried. They had been in the warehouse too long, and the guard and Richard could be discovered at any time, along with the gasoline and unwired phone they had left behind.

They came out into a space filled with plastic. Plastic covered the doors, the windows, and the walls. Inside this space, women were working in their underwear, and Alice saw one man guarding them with a machine gun. She glanced around to confirm there was only one guard, then she snuck up on him. Gesturing silently, she signaled that Kathy and Emily were to stay back. Alice rose behind the guard, and when he sensed someone was near and began to turn, she whipped her knife across his neck. He went down. She wrenched the gun from his hands before he could pull the trigger and slipped the safety on. The women stopped working. They were shocked and froze where they stood. The glazed looks on their face told a tale. The violence before them was not even penetrating their consciousness.

"Get out!" Alice told them in English. "Leave and save yourselves!"

They stared blankly at her. Looking at their appearance, she switched to Spanish. "Sal de aquí!" she said but received no response. Finally, she tried Russian, "Vykhodi, ty svoboden!"

This last command they understood. The women exchanged looks. She'd told them they were free. She waited only a moment before gesturing with the machine gun. One of them hesitantly reached for her clothes and began to leave. Alice nodded encouragingly, and the others followed suit. They were moving slowly, looking over their shoulders at Alice in fear. "Bystreye! Bystreye!" She told them to hurry.

Kathy watched as the women left and wished she could help them. A couple looked as though they'd been beaten, and she could only imagine

the conditions they had worked under in this factory. She surveyed the area where they had obviously been sorting cocaine, diluting the pure substance with other chemicals to increase their profits before placing the final mixture into little packets.

Alice was frisking the guard and found a pack of cigarettes and lighter. He hadn't dared to smoke around all these chemicals. The place was toxic, and she whispered to Kathy and a wide-eyed Emily, "Don't breathe any of this crap, if you can help :t."

They were tempted to leave by the same door the women had used, but they had something to finish first. Alice put down the gun and made her way out of the factory.

"What are you going to do with that?" Kathy whispered, gesturing to the cigarettes and lighter. She knew Alice didn't smoke.

"This will make a great fuse," she replied as she handed them to Kathy. They walked out another door and right into the path of another guard, who was holding a gun. He raised his gun, the sound of it being cocked back eerily loud in the quiet of the warehouse.

"Hold it right there!" he shouted, so he would alert his fellow guards to come to his aid. He only saw women intruders, but there might be more. He didn't recognize any of them from the crew that worked in the plastic room.

Alice raised her hands and Kathy and Emily followed suit. Kathy was looking to Alice for some sign of what she should do. She had an urge to cough but suppressed it. In one hand she held a bag filled with money, in the other she held the cigarettes and lighter handed to her by Alice. Her pack with the ledgers hung from her shoulders and over her back. Emily shifted uncomfortably as she also raised her hands, wondering what her parents would do.

"What are you doing here?" he asked while he waited for others to come. Surely, someone heard him.

"We're here to destroy your boss's operation," Alice told him, surprising all of them with her bluntness. She indicated she was going to lower her one arm, holding out her hand to show him she had nothing in it. She'd returned her knife to its sheath on her leg after she'd killed the man in the factory. Suddenly, she realized where they were standing. Her nose told her how near they were to the goods, but apparently, he couldn't smell the fumes.

"How are you going to do that?" he sneered, not believing a word she said.

"Mind if I smoke?" she asked, again flexing her fingers to show there was nothing in them.

He nodded, wishing he could have one as well. He guessed it couldn't hurt to let them smoke while they waited. He held his gun confidently, knowing they had nothing better to do than wait. *Where the hell were the others?* he wondered.

Alice took her time pulling a cigarette from the pack that Kathy handed her, then lit it and inhaled deeply to get a nice red glow on it. Alice was looking at it thoughtfully and watching the guard across the glow. Taking it in her fingers, she looked at it once more, making sure the guard's eyes were focused on it and on her, then she cocked her head as she flicked it towards the puddle of gasoline next to them. At the same time, she body-slammed Kathy and Emily, pushing them away and out of his line of fire. There was a flash as the gasoline fumes ignited. Alice continued pushing Kathy and Emily towards the exit door as the guard, distracted by the fire that was spreading rapidly along the gasoline trails, yelled in consternation. They made it out the door of the warehouse just as he

started to fire his gun, but it was too late. They were out of his line of sight, and the flames had started his clothing on fire.

"Ah, ahh, ahhhhhh!" he screamed as he desperately tried to extinguish the flames.

"Come on," Alice said, running for the SUV and holding Kathy and Emily each by an arm. Dropping her hand from Emily when they reached the street, she reached into her pants' pocket and started the vehicle remotely, unlocking it as they got closer. Finally, she released Kathy. They all jumped into the SUV. and she slammed it into drive, pulling quickly away from the warehouse. In the rear-view mirror, they could see the flames were already licking out the open door.

There was an explosion behind them, and they looked back in time to see the office go up in flames. Turning back to the front, Kathy screamed, "Look out!" and Alice swerved just barely missing the six Russian women. She breathed a sigh of relief; she had almost clipped one of them. Alice slammed on the brakes, stopped abruptly, then opened her window. Grabbing the bag of cash from Kathy's lap, she threw it at the women's feet. The bag fell open, and the cash spilled out. Alice sped off, watching in her rear-view mirror as the Russian women stopped to gather around the bag.

Alice stopped only once on the drive home to throw their gloves in a storm drain. The smell of gasoline on the gloves was overpowering.

"Now, what are we going to do with you?" Alice asked Emily, looking at her in the rear-view mirror. The pale teen glanced at Kathy, who was recovering from a coughing fit before she could turn in her seat and face her daughter.

The end, for now ;-p

K'ANNE MEINEL

If you have enjoyed **MILITARIAL MALICE**, I hope you will enjoy this excerpt from

BLOWN AWAY

There are two covers (books) available for your reading pleasure. One is more G-Rated than the other.

Don't judge a book by its cover! Nothing, and no one, is EVER what they seem.

Ellen Christenson escapes from an abusive life, but does one ever escape the scars that are left on their soul? One must move on, one must try. But life has a tendency to circle back to what one once knew, and one finds that her life choices bring her back to the scenes of her abuse to deal with it finally and fully, in ways she had never thought she would. It is then that the healing can begin, as she repairs her soul and the people she has devastated along the way.

Ellen hadn't intended to end up in Silicon Valley and its high-tech world, but due to life and its circumstances she finds herself the head of a startup tech company. Cool, calculating, efficient – she shows the world a side of her that she doesn't have, and few if any know the real Ellen. Nearby San Francisco provides her with plenty of girlfriends. That elusive one, that soulmate, she has a hard time recognizing due to the scars within.

For years, she has lived with her decision of letting someone die for their sins, and Ellen is blown away by the feelings and emotions she has bottled up for so long....

CHAPTER ONE
REMEMBRANCES

She stared at the ruins of a once beautiful farm house and memories came, flashing back in an instant yet spanning years. Over there once stood a beautiful pair of oak trees with a swing between them for her to play on. She could still hear the echoes of her mother telling her to be careful as she climbed them. Skinned knees and scraped palms; she never complained over the slivers her mother had to remove from her tomboyish activities. Their shade provided her endless hours of escape from the relentless sun and still she would burn from it. The wind would part the leaves and the sun would beat down between them. Her imagination could play for hours as she gazed up through them,

envisioning them as towering giants and she a mere mortal. She loved those trees.

"I can't believe you climb like a monkey, and in a dress too!" her mother would scold. She remembered that fondly, the inflections, the lilt in her voice was still in her consciousness despite the span of years.

The house still tilted haphazardly. Weather and time hadn't pulled it to the ground and for this she was surprised as she stared at its sturdy build. Her great-grandparents had been among the first to build in this area and had used good wood and stone to construct their sturdy home. Their son and granddaughter had both raised families in this house. She scowled as she remembered she had been the last raised in this house.

It look well picked over. The weeds around the place were elbow high and although she hadn't seen it in over twenty years, she couldn't help but wonder why it hadn't been torn down before; which was why she was now here.

"Ms. Avril?" a voice asked her respectfully and she started in surprise. She hadn't heard anyone approach. "Oh, I'm sorry miss, I was expecting…" he began apologizing.

"It's okay, you just startled me," she said in precise and clear tones, not a hint of the accent that was unique to this part of the country and so apparent in his voice. That accent brought back other memories. Ones she'd tried to quash and couldn't. Ones that she'd known needed exorcising, and *that* could only be done by coming here. It was why she had come herself. She needed to stop the dreams that had returned. Her feeling was that it was in the past and it should remain there. Her psyche though was haunting her and she had to face it, one last time.

"I was expecting Ms. Avril," he began again, and peered at her intently and wondering who she was. He was shorter than she, his skin brown from the winds that blew here; he was stooped from a lifetime of work.

She smiled, not realizing the beauty that was apparent in her face. Her pale white skin hid the freckles that came out in the sun, but no tan touched her creamy milk white skin anymore. "I'm A…Avril," she answered hesitating over the name for only a millisecond. '*Or, I was,*' she mentally corrected herself, but not aloud, he wouldn't understand.

"You're Ms. Avril?" he asked puzzled. He peered at her for a long time shaking his head, trying to see some semblance of the youth he had known. As her smile faded, he saw a glimmer of recognition. Not of her but of her mother and that was when he took on a relieved look. His hat came off his head in an instant and his weathered face wreathed a smile showing several missing teeth. "Why Ms. Avril, you've all growed up!" he drawled, pleased at his discovery.

"How are you, Mr. Davidson?" she asked pleasantly. The smile didn't quite reach her eyes though. Not with the memories pushing at her temples wanting her to remember, to relive them; all the while she was trying hard to once again suppress them.

"Poorly," he said honestly. "Right poorly, but I aim to do the job you is needing done. I shorely do. Just like I promised." He gestured to the truck that was parked at the end of the drive. On the trailer attached to it sat a front end loader, securely chained to its bed.

She glanced at it, then back at the house he had come to demolish. It was the town's attempt at getting rid of an 'eyesore' that had sat there empty for over two decades. Why they had decided that it needed to be

done now, she didn't know. But she was here, as requested, to get it done. Mr. Davidson had answered her call, surprised that she remembered him. He was eager to earn the money she had promised him for the job.

"Do you want to go through the house to look for anything?" he asked, as he noticed her silently staring at the house.

She shook her head. She had done her picking long ago, her few belongings in a few measly boxes and trunks, and a storage unit she had come to go through as well, a lifetime of memories and knick knacks that meant nothing to anyone but herself. "Just bulldoze it," she said shortly, wanting it taken care of so she could leave.

"You'll have to move your car," he mentioned, as they turned to head back down the driveway.

She glanced at the Maserati and nearly laughed aloud at the contrast between it and his old rusted out Chevy. She hadn't thought of that when she decided to drive back here. If she hadn't before, she would surely stick out like a sore thumb now. Another reason to get the job finished and get out, get gone. Something she had done years ago and not looked back. She glanced over at the barns and silos. They still looked as solid as the day her great-grandparents and grandparents had built them. Nothing had touched them, not time, nor weather, they seemed to be as strong and steady as the day they were built. They could use a little paint, but with the weather that came through this part of the country it was amazing they were still standing. She could see they were used well by the tracks that led from the path up to them and down the driveway, but that was all. Everything else was abandoned, the chicken coop, and a few other outbuildings. The grass overgrown

and obviously untrodden, no animals or people to grind it under their heels.

"Can you tear down those too?" she asked as she gestured to the outbuildings not in use.

"Ahyup," he grunted as they reached her overpriced car and she automatically pressed the button on her keychain to open the door and let her in. He glanced at the car as the door opened quietly and on its own for her, expensive enough to pay a couple of year's salary to someone like him, and most folks around here. It was none of his business though so he hurried over to the trailer where another man stood, awaiting orders. "Let's get her down," he gestured to him, and they immediately began removing the chains holding the machine to the bed of the trailer.

The younger man kept watch out of the corner of his eye as the redhead drove the expensive sports car onto the road. She parked it opposite the driveway so they could drive the front end loader onto the property. She was definitely worth a second *and* third look and he wondered if she remembered him as she watched his uncle maneuver the heavy machine off the trailer. She caught him staring as she got out of the car and he felt his cheeks reddening. He hurried after his uncle to collect any boards worth salvaging hoping she hadn't noticed. She had said they could take whatever they wanted.

She followed along slowly and looked down at her Prada shoes knowing she should have dressed down for the farm, but after twenty years she had nothing appropriate to wear on such a place. She hadn't thought about it as the miles passed and she headed for this part of Oklahoma.

CHAPTER TWO
THE ESCAPE

She remembered, vividly, the reverse trip. She had run away from here as fast as the bus would take her. Was she running away from her past or running to her future? She didn't know, but getting away from South Oklahoma had seemed like the best thing to her to do. Her bags were packed; Mrs. Davidson had agreed to send on the few boxes and trunks when she was set.

"All set?" Sheriff Worley asked, as he gave her a lift to the bus stop.

"Yep," she answered. She was frightened out of her mind but she knew she had no choice but to go. She had to leave it all behind her. Leave the memories, the only home she'd ever known, the problems, and let time fade it all.

He glanced at the young girl; he could see how scared she was. He knew he would be at her age. She was just a week over eighteen, and had signed all the papers renting out the farm to the co-op to be used as they saw fit, to farmers who wanted to use the land and the sturdy barns and silos that still stood on the property. He didn't blame her for leaving, there was nothing left. It wasn't a good time to sell, it never was, not in this economy. Farming was a gamble at the best of times; this wasn't the best of them. She had lost in so many ways, leaving was about the only option. Maybe some time away would do her good. Some of the boys who went off to school returned a little wiser, some didn't last, few stayed away for good. He was sure he'd see her back. Small town girls were worse than small town boys for wanting to return

to what was familiar, what they knew. There were a few boys around her age and a little older who would gladly marry her. She might be scrawny but she had the farm and that would draw them like bees to honey.

He didn't know her though. Avril Christenson might have died that day a couple of weeks back, instead of her father. At least in her own mind she had. Not that day, but the week before. They said lightening couldn't strike twice in the same place. They were wrong. Tornadoes did it, lightening did it too. This time though, the tornado had taken her life in this world, and left her with the shell of the person that was escaping on a bus. Everyone thought her grief was over her father but it wasn't. It was for the young woman who had been caught in her Chevy truck the week before. The woman had been her best friend and allowed Avril to be brave in the face of a dismal future. She was the one who had given Avril hope. She tried not to remember how much she had loved her best friend, how much they had planned, how much she had wanted to....

"Here we are, now you want some help buying your ticket?" the sheriff offered helpfully, as he would have any young woman.

"No thank you Sheriff Worley, I've got it," she said in a flippant, teenage way. She threw her red hair back over her shoulder, her freckles standing out in relief against her tanned face, the sun making the freckles seem unending. "Thank you for the ride," she remembered to say politely, as her mother would have wanted her to.

"No problem. Now you take care, ya'hear?" he spoke in return and watched as she gathered her backpack and two duffels and headed into the office that doubled as a bus stop and cafe. He watched through the

door and looked around to see if any undesirables were loafing about. He didn't want this young girl hassled. He would have treated her as a daughter, as any young thing in this area would be treated. Poor young thing to lose her best friend and father within a week of each other, and have to graduate high school all alone, no relatives, no close friends to see her off. Mrs. Davidson had been kind enough to take her in these last few weeks until she graduated, but other than that Avril Christenson was on her own. Maybe she was better off. That best friend of hers had been nothing but a troublemaker since she was born, with unnatural leanings from what he had observed. He had never caught her at anything, but a person knew about such things. He thought her interest in the young Avril a tragedy in the making. It had only been a matter of time until she corrupted that innocent child. Maybe God had taken her for that reason, to prevent it. That poor child, with a father like Owen Christenson to have been left with nothing like that. It was best that she leave, at least for now.

Avril knew the Sheriff was watching her, he couldn't help himself, nosy bugger that he was. She bought a one-way ticket to California, and when the clerk asked if she wanted the return ticket, she declined. The clerk had graduated from the same high school the year before and couldn't blame her for leaving and not coming back, she wished she could do it. She knew who Avril Christianson was, everyone knew. The tragedy had been all over Oakley. Losing her father like that, the poor child, and right before graduation and her eighteenth birthday, such a loss. The clerk watched her as she sat down on one of the benches for the bus that was due in at any time. Avril looked out and saw the sheriff's car was still there, waiting to see if she got on the bus

so that his 'obligation' to the citizens of this small town was discharged. She suspected he was afraid she would stay and expose him for the lecherous fool he was, a drinking buddy of her fathers, who hadn't protected her from his abuse. The many scars on her soul she laid firmly at her father's feet, but that man outside waiting in the sheriff's car could have prevented some of them after her mother's death.

It hadn't been her fault that her mother had been 'poorly' after giving birth to a 'girl child' instead of the much anticipated son and heir. That she couldn't have any more children had been blamed solely on Avril, as she had been told over and over throughout her life. Her mother tried to make up for it by shielding her from her father's abuse while she was alive, but he wore her down, he killed her slowly and surely until the shell of the woman blew away in the Oklahoma winds. Her death had been laid firmly at the young Avril's feet, and she was made to feel the abuse that her mother had shielded her from for so long. She was to take over all the duties of running a household. At ten, this was too much for any child. Farm work is tough on a woman at any given time but for a child with no one to teach her; she faltered at every turn. Only her friendship with Ellie had given her hope. Ellie implanted a fierce hope that gave her a will and strength to survive to escape her father's tyranny.

She learned to do her chores quickly and if not perfect, to hide the flaws so that she would have time to meet Ellie out on the prairie to escape his notice for a few minutes every day. She shared all her girlhood dreams with the older girl. With four years separating them, Ellie seemed worldly and wise. She understood without being told

what was happening to the smaller and younger girl. She saw the bruises and scratches from the belt she had been given for not finishing her 'work' in a timely manner or not up to his expectations. Many times his rage was fueled by liquor; he had no idea of his strength as he yelled at the youngster.

Avril put aside her memories for a moment as she watched the bus come in and one person get off. It looked bigger than the school bus she had ridden to school for nine years. She bravely got up from the bench and gathered her things, her most cherished possessions in two bags and a backpack, the rest in storage at the Davidsons, for how long she didn't know, but it couldn't be long as they were charging her for keeping it there. It was their way of profiting from having to 'keep' the minor and not getting enough cut of the deal as she had turned eighteen this past week. Had she not been so close to turning eighteen, they would have been appointed her guardians, and stolen every dime from her parent's small estate. She slowly approached the bus with her ticket in hand, and the driver leapt off the bus.

"Two bags miss?" he asked respectfully, as he opened the massive storage container underneath the bus. She nodded as he took one bag and gently put it inside the bin, and then reached for her second one closing the doors behind the bag. She must have looked worried as he said, "They'll be safe in there." She nodded with a tremulous smile.

"Ticket please?" he asked, as she hesitated to head for the door of the bus. She handed it to him as she adjusted her overly full backpack on her shoulder. He looked it over, surprised to see the destination, and handed it back to her. "You first," he said politely and indicated the stairwell. With a last look over her shoulder at the station and the

sheriff car sitting there, she went up the stairs and looked for an empty seat, one where she could watch the container if it were opened up again. All her things were in those bags, she couldn't afford to have them stolen. Sitting down, she put her backpack on the empty seat beside her, to discourage anyone from sitting next to her. She glanced around making sure not to make eye contact with anyone, and noticed the bus was barely full. A few people in the back seemed to be traveling together, but most were sitting by themselves like she was. She was close enough to the front to watch for her stuff, and to the driver in case anyone wanted to start something. She watched as he closed the door, as he sat down and strapped himself in. She looked for seat belts, but there were none, just like on the school bus. She had often wondered at that, the bus driver had once explained that in the event of an accident, that it was so the driver could get the kids out easier. She hoped a bus this large didn't get into accidents. As the bus pulled away from the depot, she saw the sheriff's car pulling away in the opposite direction, a small cloud of dust blown up from the tires. She guessed she was no longer Sheriff Worley's concern.

At first she watched the familiar landscape go by as the bus picked up speed and headed for the Interstate. It would take a while as there were several small towns such as hers that it would have to stop in. Sometimes, someone would get on, but not always. Sometimes it was a total waste of time. They had to stop though apparently, from what she could see. The landscape gradually began to change, and once they were on the Interstate it went by rapidly and she gulped, she had never been this far from home and she knew she had to be brave. A lot would change now, there was no going back. The hands of fate had been

turning for weeks now and she would be brave. She was going on: Ellie would have wanted her to, for both of them.

That was the day Avril began to go by her middle name Ellen. To honor her mother who had also been named Ellen, and it was close enough to Ellie, that it was to honor her as well. She gulped, remembering Ellie's sweet face and the plans they had made, together. They had just been waiting for her to graduate high school and turn eighteen. They had *so many* plans. Ellie had saved up enough for both of them, by working at the gas station, to start over somewhere else. The two of them against the world. They had been ready; they were just waiting for the right time.

Her father must have sensed she was getting ready to leave. His drinking had never been worse. His abuse had only increased. He felt he owned her. She was *his* child and she had to do what *he* said, his sense of ownership was truly distorted. Her turning eighteen though must have bothered him as it came closer and closer, and he started getting meaner, if that were possible. He didn't approve of Ellie May Fredericks, those 'white trash' Fredericks that lived in the mobile home trailer park. They were *better* than anyone living in a trailer park. He had told Avril often enough to stay away from *her*. The rumors about that girl were positively unnatural. He had laughed when he heard that the tornado had ripped through the trailer park where the Fredericks had lived and killed not only Ellie, but many other 'white trash.' He thought he was better than anyone living in a tornado magnet as he called mobile homes. He owned a home, he had a farm, he was better than anyone in that part of their small town.

Avril had been the one to identify Ellie, when the body was found along with her truck. Only her short yet beautiful honey blonde hair identified her with its shaved sides and the designs scored in them. Avril had run her fingers through it just the night before Ellie had been caught in the tornado, pulling into the park just as the storm hit. She had never had a chance to run to the bunker that was in the center of the park for the residents. The terror that she must have felt when the twister sucked up her Chevy must have been horrifying, her face, now at peace, still had remnants of the dirt and debris that had embedded under her skin. The rescue workers that had found her hadn't bothered to clean her up, and Avril had been hard pressed not to throw up at the sight of her beloved best friend and what nature had done to her. She left the 'temporary' morgue after identifying Ellie, and headed right for the mobile home park. The mobile home that Ellie had lived in was off its blocks and on its side, but she crawled in anyway with one look around to see if anyone had seen her. She knew scavengers would be arrested, but they would be through if she didn't get to Ellie's things first.

She crawled through the debris to find the 'safe place' that Ellie used to hide her money and most treasured things. She found the box after a long search through all the jumble. She was relieved to find the rolls of bills and the various trinkets in the box. She cried when she found the engagement ring she had known Ellie wanted to give her, but was waiting until she was 'legal.' She looked around the room and took a sweatshirt she found, but other than that she left everything as it was and crawled out of the trailer. She was just in time as she took off from the other scavengers coming into the park who would be looking

for anything they could find and sell. Supposedly 'looking' for bodies, any money or jewelry 'found' would disappear. She hid the box among her own things, hoping to keep it from being discovered by her father.

Owen Christenson didn't care about anything, but what he could find in the bottom of a gin bottle. If his friends distilled something a little more than one hundred percent proof, well that was fine by him too. When he saw her after the death of her best friend, he laughed and told her she was 'better off' without that 'trailer trash' and now she could go find a 'real man.' He even offered to find her one. She shuddered in distaste, but knew better than to answer. Around her father she was shy, she was quiet and respectful, she was non-visible as much as possible to the man. She kept his house as much as she could and waited for the day when she could leave. She had promised her mother that she would graduate high school, something she herself hadn't had the advantage of, and regretted her whole life. She wanted to keep from his notice, and the idea of his 'friends,' who looked at her with barely disguised lust, made her disgusted. Lecherous hands had reached out to her as she fetched beer for his 'friends' for years. He never stopped them, never defended her. She had learned to avoid them, for if she ever complained or spilled the beer, her father would berate her. Words were almost worse than the physical beatings, as he harangued her for 'fun' in front of those friends, much to their mutual amusement. Egged on by their silent appreciation of his abuse and his particular style of child rearing.

She watched the telephone poles loop up and down as the sun went down and she headed into it. She was heading west. Far, far away from the devastation of the two tornadoes that had hit this section of

Oklahoma in one week's time. Ellen couldn't help but wonder if her father would still be alive if she had woken him when she heard the tornado sirens go off. She had heard them loud and clear across the prairie miles from her bedroom and headed for the stairs to head for shelter. He had been asleep on the couch wearing his 'wife beater' t-shirt, appropriately named since he had always worn such disgusting shirts to beat not only his wife, but his daughter as well. He was snoring loudly, and she debated briefly about waking him, knowing she would be backhanded for 'bothering' him, but also knowing that the sirens were going loud and clear and that they should head for the shelter her grandparents had built to protect the humans from this very thing. He drooled in his sleep as his hand came up to rub his crotch and then up to rub his nose. She shuddered in disgust at the sight. The sirens must be spinning around as they came louder and then fainter, it was the next circuit that decided it for her, and she headed to the shelter, *alone.*

It was hard for her small frame to open the door; it was a heavy steel door. The wind was blowing so hard she nearly lost her footing as she struggled with it. She could see the vent spinning around on top of the storm shelter to let in some air to the close quarters. It was built tough, but she managed to pry it open, the wind catching it, before she was pulling it shut behind her and bolting it. She was in absolute darkness and she reached for a flashlight she knew they kept on the shelf. Something soft brushed against her hand, she didn't know if was a spider web, a mouse, or what, and she squealed at the sensation, but determinedly felt for the flashlight against the eternal blackness that was before her. She wouldn't go down the steps without seeing where

she was going. It was a black pit, a void, an absence of any light, and she was frightened. She had heard the roar of the wind, the steel door had shut that out, but in the absence of sound the dark frightened her further. There, there was the flashlight. She quickly pulled it to herself and flicked it on. The beam was feeble, the batteries old and unused. She cursed in her mind, not aloud, just in case someone could hear her and berate her for her naughty mouth. She shone the flickering beam around and saw another flashlight on the shelf. This one too was weak and unused, but between the two weak beams she felt better and could see further. She saw a lantern further down and headed carefully down the stairs. The noises outside as things hit the door scared her, she wondered how long she would have to stay down here, she wondered if she should go back up and get her father. Remembering how he had laughed at Ellie's death, seeming to take pleasure in the devastation on his young daughters face, she firmly decided that he was on his own. He would make her pay in countless ways later, but she knew it was a price she had to pay.

She got the lantern lit and it provided much more light than the weak flashlights that she turned off. The wind could be heard around the steel door and a little gray through the small window in the door, but nothing she could see beyond an absence of black through it. She looked around the storm cellar. Her grandparents and even her mother had stored things in here, but her father never did, he didn't even use it, only swore that he had to cut around it in the backyard with the lawn mower. Occasionally she jumped as something fell against the door or window; she could sense the power of the wind.

Oh no! She remembered the box she had taken from Ellie's home; she had forgotten it in her hiding place in her room. It was all she had to start over! She got up for a moment with the intention of heading back to the house, but a loud crash outside the storm door had her halting in her tracks.

TO BE CONTINUED...

Check out all my books at: www.kannemeinel.com.

About the Author

K'Anne Meinel is a Lesbian Fiction bestselling author with more than 100 published works including shorts, novellas, and novels. She is an American author born in Milwaukee, Wisconsin and raised in Oconomowoc. Upon early graduation from high school she went to a private college in Milwaukee and then moved to California for seventeen years before returning to the state. Many of her stories have Wisconsin in them as settings for her wonderful, realistic, and detailed backgrounds. Named the lesbian Danielle Steel of her time, K'Anne continues to write interesting stories in a variety of genres in both the lesbian and mainstream fiction categories.

What do you do when you meet someone who changes everything you know about love and passion?

Paige Harlow is a good girl. She's always known where she was going in life: top grades, an ivy league school, a medical degree, regular church attendance, and a happy marriage to a man. So falling in love with her gorgeous roommate and best friend Alyssa Torres is no small crisis. Alyssa is chasing demons of her own, a medical condition that makes her an outcast and a family dysfunctional to the point of disintegration make her a questionable choice for any stable relationship. But Paige's heart is no longer her own. She must now battle the prejudices of her family, friends, and church and come to peace with her new sexuality before she can hope to win the affections of the woman of her dreams. But will love be enough?

~ Because a publisher should stand behind their authors~

When Delaney Delacroix is called to locate a missing girl, she never plans on getting caught up with a human trafficking investigation or with the local witch. Meeting with Raelin Montrose changes her life in so many ways that Delaney isn't sure that this isn't destiny.

Raelin Montrose is a practicing Wiccan, and when the ley lines that run under her home tell her that someone is coming, she can't imagine that she was going to solve a mystery and find the love of her life at the same time.

Amelia Gittens had the credit of being the first and only woman thus far in the United States military of being a sniper in combat, made possible by being in the Military Police unit of the crack 10th Mountain Infantry Division. After retirement she joins the City of New York Police Department, and suddenly finds herself involved in a suspect shooting incident which soon encroaches upon her entire life. In order to protect her therapist who has been targeted as a revenge killing, Amelia takes on the responsibility as if she was still in the Army, treating it as a tactical maneuver.

An abused and bullied teenager is suddenly granted great and terrible powers by an ancient goddess. Each step towards womanhood is shaped by her new abilities, as is the woman she will become. Devil or angel, which will she be? Will the woman who chases her ever know for sure?

Both men tried to shoot her then, and the two women were stunned at the speed with which she moved. Penny charged straight at the gunmen then dove under their fire. Spinning on her back she kicked the legs from under one man, and as he fell, she kicked the gun from the other man's hand. Spinning back to the first man she saw the gun barrel moving toward her, and she lashed out with her foot. Her boot crushed his skull and she rolled to her feet to grab the last man in a neck lock. A quick twist and he lay lifeless in her arms.

She let him fall, as, breathing deeply, she came down off combat mode. "Are you ladies all right?" she asked as she untied the ropes that held the older woman.

"Who are you?" asked the old woman fearfully, as she pulled the tape from her mouth.

"They call me Lady Blue," smiled Penny as she helped the woman to stand.

"What are you?" It was the younger woman who spoke.

"Cold, hungry, dead tired, and covered in blue war paint," giggled Penny as she released the older woman's arm. She turned and began to search the bodies.

If you have enjoyed this book and the others listed here Shadoe Publishing is always looking for first, second, or third time authors. Please check out our website @ www.shadoepublishing.com For information or to contact us @ shadoepublishing@gmail.com.

We may be able to help you make your dreams of becoming a published author come true.